RESET

RESET

Ordinary People, Extraordinary Events.

TIMOTHY BENSON

iUniverse LLC
Bloomington

Reset
Ordinary People, Extraordinary Events

iUniverse books may be ordered through booksellers or by contacting:

iUniverse LLC
1663 Liberty Drive
Bloomington, IN 47403
www.iuniverse.com
1-800-Authors (1-800-288-4677)

ISBN: 978-1-4917-0548-3 (sc)
ISBN: 978-1-4917-0550-6 (hc)
ISBN: 978-1-4917-0549-0 (ebk)

Library of Congress Control Number: 2013915912

Printed in the United States of America

iUniverse rev. date: 08/29/2013

DEDICATION

To my daughters, Stephanie and Alyson, and their families, who are a constant reminder to me to live in the future and not the past.

"Whatever You Say"

Blasdell, NY

Matt used his left hand to pull his jacket collar closer to his neck while he held the gasoline nozzle with his right. Squinting into the icy wind, he tried to see the read-out on the gas pump. He wanted to make sure he filled his tank as full as possible because the first leg of his route to Atlanta would leave him somewhere in Ohio by the time he had to stop for the night. The winter storm was hugging the Lake Erie shoreline, and it would be at least a couple of hours before he got far enough south to drive out of it.

The pump nozzle clicked at the full mark but Matt knew he could squeeze at least another gallon into his aging Explorer. He shivered as he watched the read out jerk along, alternately squeezing and releasing the handle, and he wondered if he would ever again have to deal with horrible winter weather. If growing up in the Buffalo area had taught him one thing, it was that winter lasted for six months no matter what happened the rest of the year. His decision to leave his hometown was bittersweet for a variety of reasons, but part of him wished he had left years ago, before he had settled into a rut. One thing was certain though, the miserable weather made it easier to leave.

When he knew the tank was as full as he could get it, he hung up the nozzle and hurried through the snowy parking lot into the Country Fair. A large coffee and donut would keep him going for a while.

While he was filling the paper cup a man at the other end of the counter looked over and asked, "How do you people around here put up with this damn weather?"

Matt hesitated, unable to come up with a positive response he could be sincere about, or even believe himself. He answered, "Beats me, I'm not from around here myself." *Okay, I know that's a lie but since I'm leaving town I guess it's sort of true.*

The man smiled, "They tell me that around here they call this shit *lake-effect snow* and they can have every damned inch of it."

"Yeah, I hear yah man," Matt said, "I'm from New York . . . City and heading south. This kind of weather is all new to me." *Hmm, another little fib but it sounds believable I guess.* He carefully put the lid on his cup and looked over the donut selection.

"I'm heading to New York myself," the stranger continued. "so how long until I drive out of all this snow?"

Matt dropped a thick glazed donut into a bag. "I got all the way to Elmira before I ran into anything heavy, so you have about forty-five minutes or so until you'll see anything close to dry pavement. *That's just what I heard on the radio an hour ago.*

"So what do you do in New York?" the man asked.

"I write music, mostly for commercials, but some stuff for theatre too." *Yeah, I still remember that song I did for the junior class play in high school.*

"What commercials, anything I might have heard?"

"Probably not, I do mostly local stuff. I did one for Jiffy Lube and one for a chain of car dealers. It pays the bills until the theatre work pays off. Hopefully, I can score a movie someday." *Wow, this sounds way more interesting than my real career. I wish it was all true.*

Matt turned and headed to the register and the man grabbed his own coffee and followed. "Wow, that's really cool," he said. "What's your name? I'll keep my eye on the movie credits. Maybe I'll see it up on the screen someday."

"It's Matt, Matt Bingham"

"Okay, nice talking to you Matt Bingham," the stranger replied.

Matt said, "Nice talking to you too, drive safe," and headed back out the door. He hurried through the snow flurries and climbed on to the seat of his truck. After he started it up he looked back into the rear hatch and backseat, both packed full with every single thing that was important enough to take along on his journey. He was nearly 30 years old and his entire lot of worldly possessions fit inside a 2005 Ford Explorer; two pieces of beat up luggage, six boxes of clothes, a few books, audio equipment, a small TV, a laptop computer and two guitars. Not exactly a fortune but, then, anything more would only slow him down. "It's like Dad always says," he thought to himself, "life is portable."

As he adjusted his rearview mirror and saw his reflection he was reminded that he hadn't shaved that morning, and he looked more than a little scruffy. He was used to a work routine that required business attire, shined shoes and good grooming. For the next few days he'd have the freedom to relax the rules for a change. Totally alone and totally on his own, and, he hoped, on his way to something better.

He pulled out into the light morning traffic and in a few minutes he reached the entrance ramp to Interstate 90 West. He sipped his coffee, wolfed down his donut and thought again about why he was heading to Atlanta. He had been thinking about his future a lot over the past year, and his October break-up with his long-time girlfriend, Dena, seemed like a signal that it was time to make a change. His life had long ago settled into a dull routine of a boring job in an asset management and investment office, hanging out with the same group of sports-obsessed friends at the same two bars and trying to convince himself that Dena's desire to get married made some kind of sense. His parents had retired to Florida and his sister moved to Connecticut. The western New York economy had all but killed the job market. His business degree from Saint Bonaventure was probably broad enough to help him find a job but not deep enough to make it pay any more money than what he was already making. And all of the events of his life played out in what seemed to be never ending snow and rain.

He decided not to rush this trip to his new life. His cousin Dan was waiting for him and had a spare room that he offered to Matt until he could find a place of his own. He and Dan were close in age and Dan said he knew a few people he could introduce him to who could help him find a job somewhere. Growing up together, Matt always envied Dan's ability to make friends and take charge, and he hoped that would translate to help in finding him an opportunity in Atlanta. He was trying to be optimistic and maintain his "what have I got to lose?" attitude, but he also worried that he would just end up in the same rut in a place that had better weather. All in all, not much of a step forward. Then he thought about the line of bullshit that he spewed to the man at the convenience store. **A music writer from the Big Apple.** He had no idea why he said those things. Even though he liked to joke around a lot, it wasn't normal for him to make up stories like that, but he had to admit that he enjoyed it. Normally he went out of his way to avoid small talk like that, but for some reason today he felt like indulging in a little bit of fantasy. He was leaving his old life and looking for something new, and for a few minutes a total stranger had given him the chance to be someone new., a traveling artist instead of a sedentary pencil pusher. He kind of liked that idea.

Mason, OH

Even though the snow had stopped hours ago when he turned south on to I-271, Matt was still relieved when he saw the Holiday Inn sign glowing in the darkness. He had skipped lunch so he could make sure he was clear of the bad weather before he stopped for the night. A good meal and a drink or two would be a good finish to the first day of his new life. He managed to find a parking space near the front door then set about digging through the back of the Explorer to grab the things he'd need for the night. He slipped the strap of his day bag over his shoulder and set his two guitar cases on the pavement while he closed the hatch. He had considered selling his guitars before he left because he didn't play them much anymore. Three years of lessons during high school, an attempt at making his little garage band into something real, and the occasional pot-fueled solo performances in his college apartment didn't exactly make him a virtuoso. He had always loved playing and had the same fantasies of rock stardom shared by every young male guitarist. Dena never gave him much encouragement to stay with his music and he always found an excuse of his own to leave the guitars in their cases instead of his hands. For some unexplained reason he just couldn't give them up. Maybe it was because they were part of his youth, and, because they were worth a fair amount of money, he couldn't leave them in a cold car in the winter and risk damage to the veneers.

He checked in at the front desk, went up to his room long enough to drop his stuff and use the bathroom and then headed back down to the lounge. *The Starlighter Lounge* was the typical hotel-chain bar and restaurant; a little too dark, a little too glitzy and a whole lot too noisy. He found a stool at the end of the bar and looked around the half-filled room.

"Hi there, my name is Megan and I'll be your server this evening, what can I get for you?"

Matt turned and saw a very cute young woman with short brown hair and a dazzling, expensive looking smile.

"Hi," he said, answering her smile with one of his own, "what do you have on tap?"

Megan rattled off a very short list of domestic beers and two imports. Matt was a lover of microbrews but had already prepared himself to accept something less in taste and imagination if necessary. "Sam Adams Winter Lager," he said, trying to keep his flirtation from looking too obvious.

About a minute later Megan returned and set a full pint glass in front of him. She smiled and said, "I was in the lobby and saw you check in with the guitars. Are you a musician?"

Wow, this girl is perceptive. "Yes, I am, I play guitar, dobro and occasionally some pedal steel." *Okay man, there's no way she knows what dobro and pedal steel mean.*

"Oh wow, you do country. Are you in a band?"

I stand corrected she's a country music buff. "No I'm mostly a session musician. I do back-up guitar for a lot of people in recording studios and whenever they need me."

Matt looked around at his fellow patrons, wondering if anyone else could hear his little fantasy story. Megan stood directly in front of him, her blue eyes wide with interest.

"Do you do any concert stuff?" she asked.

Uh-oh, looks like I'll have to come up with something good. "Well, as a matter of fact I did a tour in England last summer with Lonestar."

Megan's eyes seemed to light up. "Oh my God, really?"

Oh shit, I picked a band she actually knows. "Yeah, we played four cities in five days. They love American country music over there." *Man, you have no clue if that's even true.*

"Yeah, I know, so are you, like, friends with the band?"

"Well, I don't know if you could call us friends, but Richie McDonald and I closed a few pubs during the tour." *Good thing I read Rolling Stone once in a while.*

"Tell you what, "Megan said, "this round is on me."

"Gee, that's very nice of you," Matt replied. *Man, I think I found a freakin' country music groupie here.*

He pulled a menu from a rack on the bar and started searching for something filling and reasonably healthy.

"Excuse me." the man a few stools down from him interrupted. "I couldn't help but overhear your conversation."

Matt looked at the man and thought how totally out of place he looked to be sitting at a small town hotel bar. The guy was tall, handsome, with dark hair and piercing brown eyes and he was impeccably dressed. He looked like he'd stepped right out of GQ Magazine. Matt also noticed that the man had the oddest sounding British accent he'd ever heard.

The man leaned back and gestured toward the elegant and attractive brunette seated beside him. "My friend Elizabeth and I are just back from London, and we were wondering where you and your friends performed while you were there."

Oh shit, I don't know a damn thing about London. What was that place they mentioned in Rolling Stone? "Well, "he answered, struggling to remember what he had read about the tour. *Wait, Springsteen is going to play at Hyde Park.* "We did two shows at Hyde Park, not exactly as big as Royal Albert Hall." *The George Harrison memorial concert DVD in my collection.* "But it was a great place to play." Megan had returned and was standing in front of Matt, hanging on every word.

The man with the odd accent nodded, "Yes, it's a beautiful place and the acoustics are wonderful."

Matt nodded in agreement. "Yeah, we were surprised how little we needed to amp things up in a place that big." *Geez, I sound like a damned roadie.*

Between sipping his beer and ordering his dinner, Matt formally introduced himself to the couple. "Hi, I'm Matt . . . Cale." *Yeah, J.J. Cale, my favorite guitar player of all time, my guitar God.*

The man introduced himself as John Higgins and told Matt he was from Dartford, near London. He had been in the Cincinnati area for three days of meetings with a large semiconductor manufacturer that his company was planning to purchase. The young, long legged and beautiful Elizabeth was from New York and was accompanying John on his trip. She sat on the barstool, wearing a short black dress, legs crossed, looking aloof and altogether stunning.

Matt ordered a steak sandwich platter and another beer, gave Megan a thorough and lingering look-over as she walked away, then he turned back toward Higgins. They made the usual barroom small talk and John told Matt about his friend, Alan. John bragged about Alan's talent as a musician and his desire to carve out a musical career. As they talked Matt squirmed nervously and wondered where the conversation was leading.

John leaned closer toward him, almost eliminating the one-barstool gap between them. "Matt," he said "Alan is a very talented young man, but he doesn't know anything about the music business. Do you suppose if he contacted you, you could find some time to speak with him?"

Oh shit, there it is. Help his friend get into a line of work I'm not really into myself. "Well, I suppose I could talk to him, but I'm on my way to Nashville and I'll be tied up for quite a while. *Well, I'm driving through Nashville on my way to Atlanta so it's sort of true. Geez, where is this little conversation going?*

Higgins reached into the breast pocket of his gray suit and pulled out a small leather-bound notepad. He tore off a sheet of paper, handed it to Matt and asked him to write down his phone number so Alan could contact him. For a moment Matt considered writing down a phony number, but then reluctantly scrawled his fake name and the number for his cellphone. *No way his friend is ever going to call me . . . I hope.*

"Thank you so much," John said as he tucked the paper into his wallet.

For the next half hour Matt worked on eating his meal and carrying on a conversation about his fake career as a musician.

Megan seemed to stay close by as Matt spun one line of bullshit after another. The long hours in the studio with Faith Hill trying to get his dobro part strong enough to carry the melody. His budding friendship with Dierks Bentley, who insists that Matt be part of everything he records. And the time it took almost two whole days to record a three minute song with Carrie Underwood. *Man, be careful, you're laying it on pretty thick.* He couldn't help but notice the look in Megan's eyes as he talked. *You know, this is all bullshit but I have to admit it's kind of fun.*

When he realized he was going on and on too long about himself, he asked John about the companies he was planning to buy. As John explained the plan for the purchase, Matt felt right at home with the conversation. Acquisitions were a big part of what he had been working on during the past two years at Investar. Even though they were mostly deals for small, local and regional companies Matt enjoyed the wheeling and dealing that went along with it. John's situation was global in scale and Matt was dying to know more without sounding like he actually knew the business. After all, *Matt Cale* was just a country guitar player.

After a long and somewhat smug sounding explanation of the way his company viewed the global economy, John glanced down at his very expensive looking watch and exclaimed, "Oh my, its nearly ten." He turned to Elizabeth. "Darling, we have to be on the road early tomorrow to catch our flight out of Cincinnati." John waved to Megan and asked for the check while Matt finally got to speak, albeit briefly, with the lovely but quiet Elizabeth. Finally, the three of them exchanged good-byes and as he walked away John reminded Matt that Alan would be in touch with him soon. *Oh God, please make him lose my phone number.* Matt watched them leave then turned back to his beer, just as Megan walked down the bar and stood in front of him, smiling. "They are really nice people", he said.

"Yes they are", Megan answered, "so nice that they paid for your dinner."

Matt immediately felt embarrassed for misleading them. He knew there was no way he could ever help Higgins' friend get into the music business, and he assumed that's why they were generous enough to pay his tab.

Megan looked at him with a wink and a flirtatious smile. "Well, Matt Cale, you sure know how to make friends."

There was enough daylight streaming through a small gap in the draperies to awaken Matt long before he had planned to get up. Part of him wanted to roll over and go back to sleep but a bigger part remembered his plan to make it to Nashville before dark. Reality hit both parts of him when he felt Megan pressing up against his back. Her breath warmed his neck as she draped an arm over his shoulder. ***Oh shit, I almost forgot.*** He lay very still as he tried to figure out what he was going to say to her when she woke up. He hadn't had a night like this since his college days and he never learned a sensitive and decent way to handle the morning after.

Megan seemed like a very sweet young woman and he felt guilty about all of the bullshit that had gotten her interested in him. He knew a financial consultant could never have impressed her the way a professional guitarist did. ***Oh come on man, don't beat yourself up. She's old enough to make her own decisions.*** He rolled over to face her and in the process woke her up.

She opened her eyes halfway, hesitated a moment, then smiled. "Mornin'," she said softly.

"Mornin' yourself," he answered, studying her face and trying to read her mood. ***Geez, how can a woman look so beautiful so early in the morning?***

Matt looked over at the clock on the nightstand. "Oh man, it's after 7:00 and I have a lot of driving ahead of me," he said quietly. Megan's expression changed noticeably. ***Okay, here it is, the moment of truth.*** "I'm glad I met you," he said, looking straight into her beautiful blue eyes.

"Yeah, same here," she answered. After several awkward seconds passed she asked, "Last night, you gave that man your phone number. Would you give it to me too?"

Well, what's the worst that could happen? An uncomfortable call or two and then the whole thing dies a quiet death. "Of course I will, I was hoping you'd ask." *Actually, that's kind of true.*

Megan got out of bed, picked up her clothes from the chair beside the bed and Matt enjoyed the view as she walked into the bathroom. He pulled on his jeans and t-shirt and started to gather his things from the dresser. He looked for something to write his phone number on and instinctively reached for one of his old business cards in his wallet. *Whoops, that won't work. I'm a professional musician not an Acquisition Specialist.* Then, tearing a page from the little hotel notepad by the phone he wrote down his number. He remembered to write his name as *Matt Cale.* A few awkward minutes later they were standing by the door and he looked down at her as she fished around in her purse for her car keys. *Yep, definitely beautiful.*

Megan looked up at him as if waiting for him to say something. Finally, when he didn't she said, "Well, I guess I better go."

Matt smiled. "Yeah, I have to get on the road now too." He bent down to kiss her but she beat him to it, and he was surprised at the energy she put into it. Then he put the piece of paper with his number into her hand and, almost as an afterthought he said, "How about writing yours down too." He walked over to the desk and grabbed the pad and pen and handed it to her. She had a noticeable smile on her face while she wrote her number, as if his request meant something more than he intended. But then, he had no idea what he intended. She handed the paper and pen back to him as he opened the door. She kissed him again and then left, walking quickly to the elevator. He watched her until she went around the corner then closed the door and stood there for a moment, thinking about last night. *Matt Cale sure has a more interesting life than Matt Bingham.*

Louisville, KY

The drive down I-71 was uneventful and borderline boring. The sky was a constant pale grey, the bare trees were a medium gray and the highway was dark gray with darker gray patches. Matt had never learned to like winter in western New York, and except for the lack of snow and slush, Kentucky looked pretty much the same. He figured he would have to drive a lot farther to find something green or colorful.

Without anything to distract him outside his car windows it was easy to think about the events of last night. His playful change of identity from a business man to a wandering musician sure led to a memorable night. Free drinks, a free dinner and sensuous time with a beautiful woman. It had all played out just like the stories he'd read about the lives of musicians. All of the stereotypes were there. He even felt like he was transforming into something different. In his jeans and plaid shirt, with two days of growth on his unshaven face and a country station playing on the car radio, his white collar world seemed to be fading with every mile. Even the string of cellphone messages from his hometown buddies was starting to thin out. Buffalo was already feeling like part of his past.

The highway signs for Louisville were appearing more frequently and he started looking for restaurant signs. He hadn't taken time in Ohio to stop for breakfast and his hunger pangs were starting to be a distraction. There were plenty of signs for chain restaurants, but he was in the mood for local color instead of an Applebee's or McDonalds. Finally he saw one that looked interesting: Chet's Hometown Diner, two miles ahead at Exit 114. *With a name like Chet, the guy has to know some good, down-home cooking. And it's a freaking diner, not a bistro or café.* He moved into the right lane and exited. The diner was about a block down the frontage road on his right.

He pulled into the nearly empty parking lot and thought that the lack of business could be due to two things: it was nearly two o'clock and the lunch rush was long over, or the food was lousy. He hoped it was the time and not the food. The frozen ground crunched under his shoes as he walked in and took a stool at the far end of the counter. Chet's Diner looked like so many diners he had tried back in Buffalo; a long heavily worn laminate counter with red swivel stools, tables and mismatched wooden chairs strung along the long front window, ceiling tiles stained with years of roof leaks and the smell of a food selection based on all things fried. The plastic menus in the rack in front of him read "Chet's Diner"—Serving Grub & Grins Since 1965." *Well, I wanted local color and it looks like I found it.* He looked over the lunch offerings, hoping to find something reasonably healthy but he was realistic enough to know that nobody had ever figured out how to make hot dogs, chiliburgers and fried egg sandwiches in a way that was anything close to healthy.

A sturdily built, gray haired woman walked through the door from the kitchen and approached Matt. "Hi sugar, how y'all doin' this afternoon?" she asked in a cigarette-ravaged voice.

"Oh, I'm doin' just fine, ma'am," he answered. *Might as well try to sound like a Southerner like everybody else.*

The woman smiled and said, "Ain't seen you in here before, you just passin' through?"

"Yes, ma'am, headin' back home to Nashville." *Think I'll stay in* Matt *Cale mode awhile longer.*

The woman said, "My sister lives in Nashville, Hannah Marston, maybe you know her."

Good Lord, there's gotta be over half a million people in Nashville *and I'm supposed to know her sister.* "No ma'am, I'm afraid I don't know her."

"She's my little sister actually, lived in Nashville for goin' on twenty years."

Fascinating.

"Oh well, what can I get for yah, sugar?"

He had resigned himself to eating the kind of lunch that he normally tried to avoid. "Well ma'am, I'll have the fried egg sandwich on whole wheat."

"Only comes on white."

"Okay, on white, and I'd like a side salad with that."

"Comes with French fries or onion rings, have to charge you for a salad."

"That's fine, can I get a low-fat dressing on the side?"

"Got Italian, French or Ranch, don't know much about the fat."

Jesus, this is getting painful. "Okay, I'll take Ranch, on the side, and I'd like iced tea." *I'll bet they only have hot tea.*

"Sorry, hun, we only have hot tea, how about a Coke?"

"Sure, make it a Coke."

He got up and walked a few places down the counter and picked up a newspaper that someone had left behind, then sat back down and paged through the Local section. The news from Louisville wasn't much different than the news from Buffalo, or probably any other down-trodden city in a bad economy. He turned to the entertainment section and found an entire page of ads for Nashville concerts and events. Nashville was a little over two hours away and he figured those clubs and stages drew people from all over the Southeast. He had called ahead and made a reservation at a Marriott Hotel, and from the address the woman on the phone had given him it was on the same street as some of the music clubs he saw in the ads. *Geez, maybe Matt Cale can take in a show with his fellow guitarists.*

After about ten minutes the waitress brought him his lunch and then surrounded his plate with mustard, ketchup, salt, pepper, red pepper flakes, steak sauce and a small metal rack with four kinds of hot sauce. "Need anything else, sugar?" she asked.

Matt looked at the huge plate of fried food and the tiny little salad. "No, ma'am, I think I'm good for now." He held his sandwich in his left hand while he turned the pages of the newspaper with his right, and for some reason he found himself flipping back to the music ads every few minutes.

He ran out of interest in the newspaper about the same time he ran out of food, and as he was getting ready to pay his tab his cellphone rang. He looked at the screen and didn't recognize the number. It was from area code 283. He stared at it a moment then realized it was Megan. *Geez, what do I say? I just left her this morning.* He decided not to answer for now and figured he could call her from Nashville. *That's it, I'll call her from home, or at least that's what she'd expect.* He laid eight dollars on the counter along with his check, enough for a two dollar tip for Hannah Marston's big sister, then grabbed the newspaper and left.

He was almost to the Nashville area before he finally stopped burping memories of Chet's Diner. In the fading daylight, he looked for signs for his Marriott Hotel. He finally saw one for the downtown location on Fourth Avenue North, the one near all of the music bars and clubs. In his mind he was already tasting a cold beer. *I wonder if Matt Cale should join me tonight.*

Nashville, TN

His room was bigger and nicer than he'd expected and he laid his wheelie-bag on the jack stand and his guitars on the extra double bed. It was only 5:30 and he figured he had time to shower and shave before heading out for the evening. Standing and looking out the window over the parking lot, he popped open a can of Genesee Cream Ale from the small stash he had in the back of the Explorer. It wasn't as good as the beers he had been trying lately, but it was brewed near Buffalo and it was his beer of choice in college. He had bought a six-pack a few days before almost as an afterthought. It was just another connection to his past that he knew would soon fade away.

When he had cleaned up and gotten dressed, he looked over at the guitar cases lying on the other bed. Maybe it was all of his guitar player bullshit from the night before or the fact he was in the Music Capital of America, but something made him walk over to the bed, open the case with his Taylor 700 acoustic six-string inside, and pull it out. He held it in front of him, looking over the beautiful Spruce veneer face, Rosewood veneer accents and the long, graceful neck. It had been a gift on his eighteenth birthday and he played it and babied it all through college and his first few years of living on his own. It was an acoustic-electric design and he started out playing soft, acoustic ballads but eventually turned to more amp-driven electric riffs. For a few years that beautiful guitar was like another appendage, but it seemed like a hundred other things got in the way and it had been sleeping in its case for years.

He sat down on his bed and held it in his lap. A mother-of-pearl pick was still stuck under the strings at the top of the neck and he pulled it out and ran it gently over the strings. Even badly out of tune, he thought about how good that old Taylor sounded after all the years of being ignored. He managed to get it tuned to an acceptable level and started to play the first song that he ever played in front of other people: Nickelback's "Sea Groove". He had played it so many times he could almost do it without thinking, but now, after years of being away from the feel and touch of that old guitar, he felt more than a little rusty. He leaned back against the headboard and continued his reunion with the instrument. Everything felt good again, the feel of his fingers on the strings, the soft tones in his ears and the vibration of every note against his chest. It was just after 7:00 when his cellphone rang and shook him out of his six-string trance.

He grabbed the phone from his nightstand and saw Megan's number again. ***Shit, I completely forgot to call her back, better not put off this conversation any longer.*** "Hello, this is Matt."

"Hey Matt, its Megan, how are you?"

Matt slid the guitar from his lap and leaned back. "Oh hi there, I'm fine, how about you?"

"Oh, okay I guess. I called you earlier but you didn't pick up."

"Yeah, I was driving and couldn't get to the phone fast enough." There was an uncomfortable pause and Matt finally said, "Well, I'm back in Nashville."

Another pause and Megan said, "I wish I was there too. Are you playing anywhere tonight?"

"Nope, not tonight, but I'm going to a club to hear some new band that wants to record something this Spring." ***In this town that's probably true.*** He waited a moment for Megan to say something, and then said, "I was thinking about you on the drive here today." ***That's definitely true.***

He noticed the change in her voice as she let out a soft laugh and said, "Well, right back at yah'."

The conversation seemed to get easier the longer they talked. Megan was thinking about a Spring-time vacation and Matt was trying to think of a way he could see her in Nashville. ***I guess I could drive up from Atlanta except she'd expect to see where I live.*** The conversation was easy and Matt was feeling very comfortable talking with a beautiful woman who he had known for only twenty-four hours. Finally, he told her that he had to get down to the club before the show started and Megan seemed to understand.

"I'd really like to see you again, Matt Cale."

Matt hesitated, reminded again of the line of bullshit that brought them together. "Yeah, I want to see you too. I'm glad you called me today." ***True again.*** "How about if I call you again in a few days after things get back to normal?" he asked her.

"Sure, I'd like that . . . anytime."

They said goodbye and Matt sat back on the bed with his phone on his lap. He reached again for his guitar and tried to remember the fingering for a song he used to play with his band. It was *Suzy Lee,* kind of a hard-edged, romantic ballad by White Stripes, his favorite garage band revival group. Somehow a song about confused romantic feelings seemed appropriate at the moment.

He left his room about eight o'clock and stopped at the front desk to confirm his hunch that the music clubs were just down the street. The man behind the desk gave him an opinion on which club was best and added, "It's the best place to see new bands and meet the agents." *Interesting I guess, if I really was Matt Cale and not Matt Bingham.* Matt thanked the man and headed for the parking lot.

The Basement Club was less than a mile from the hotel and Matt was surprised to find a parking space in a city lot behind the building next door. He walked into the dark, musty smelling lobby and showed his driver's license to the large, tattooed man standing at the entrance. "Hey, a Buffalo man," he said without looking up. "How much snow you guys gettin' this year?"

Geez, is that the only thing people think about when they think of Buffalo? "Too much," Matt replied as he tucked his license back into his wallet.

The man smiled and nodded as Matt squeezed through the bottleneck of people at the entrance into the main room. He worked his way to the bar and took a stool at the far end, his favorite part of any bar he visited. He could see the entire place but not have to be smack in the middle of the noise and the crowd. Although, the way the people were pouring through the door it looked like it would be a mob scene no matter where he sat.

He was glad to see that the bar served several ales from a local microbrewery, and he ordered a Hop Project IPA. Two young men in black tee-shirts were on the small stage setting up amps and doing sound checks. The flyers tacked on the lobby walls said the opening act was a local band called *Windblown,* and from the testimonials and their photo he figured they were a roots rock group. He had always liked Americana and folk-fused rock, and he was looking forward to hearing something fresh. At least he hoped it was fresh and not the usual cover band music that you find opening for established bands in smaller clubs. The main act was *100 Proof,* and all he knew about them was what he heard two women saying as he walked through the lobby; the band was just back from a tour in Florida and they had a new bass player who was supposed to be amazing.

As he sipped his beer and felt a hop-induced buzz coming on, he looked around and thought about why he had always liked country music. The crowd was a broad mix of twenty-somethings, couples and gray-haired guys in jeans. Nobody was trying to make a fashion statement or show off. They were here for the music and a chance to be themselves. ***Geez, I wish I would have played more country when the band was together.***

"Is this stool taken?" He turned and saw a portly man in a neatly trimmed gray beard, jeans and a herringbone sport coat standing next to him.

"Nope, it's all yours'" he answered.

The man sat down and Matt nudged his stool to the left to give the man a little more room. As he waited for the bartender to notice him, the man turned to him and said, "Rupert Bascom," and offered his hand.

Matt responded, "Matt Cale," and thought to himself that Bascom had the strongest handshake he'd encountered in a long time.

"You know this band playing tonight?" Bascom asked.

"Which one?" Matt responded.

"The openers, *Windblown,* you a fan of theirs?"

"Nope, I don't know anything about them, how about you?"

"Not a fan really, I just heard some good things and decided to check them out."

Matt was still feeling more like Bingham than Cale but talking to a real Nashville music man interested him so he decided to step up the musician façade. *What would Matt Cale be looking for tonight?* "I play guitar so I'm always hoping to find a band that respects the strings and doesn't let the vocals take over everything."

He looked over at Bascom, who was beaming ear to ear. *Uh-oh, did I say something stupid?*

"You know Matt, that's exactly how I feel too. These bands today think they have to have some angry guy or a hot babe wailing into the mike, but that just ain't music to me."

"Yep, when the lead singer doesn't have a guitar slung over his shoulder you just know you aren't gonna hear much except the vocals."

Bascom finally got to order a Scotch and water from the harried bartender, paused and asked, "So are you in a band?"

Shit, I was hoping he wouldn't go there. "Not right now. I had a band in upstate New York awhile back, doing mostly cover stuff like Nickelback and a little Coldplay." Bascom just nodded, and Matt continued. "I wanted to go more in the direction of country and roots rock but the rest of the guys wanted to go heavier and darker, so we split up. You know how that goes." *I hope that's enough of an explanation. It sure sounds believable and it's pretty much what happened.*

Bascom nodded again. "So, are you looking to get back into it? I might know a band that could use a lead guitar, especially if you don't mind steppin' out in front once in a while."

Geez, why couldn't I have heard those words ten years ago? He thought for a moment and then answered, "You know on my way down here I heard about a guy who's really a good string man, his name is Alan, maybe I should put you two in touch. *Man, should I have said that? Do I really want to get involved in a stranger's problem when I have my own stuff to deal with?*

He drained the last bit of beer and foam from his glass and waved to the bartender for another. "Well," he continued," it sounds tempting but I have to be in Atlanta tomorrow, so can I get back to you on that?"

Bascom reached into the pocket of his sport coat, pulled out a business card and handed it to Matt. *Rupert Bascom Agency* in bold blue letters, then below it, *Music Promotions & Representation.* Before either man could say anything else, the club announcer bellowed in to the microphone an introduction for the opening act. Matt leaned toward Bascom and shouted into his ear, "Rupert, in case I can't hear you again tonight, it was great talking to you, and I will definitely think about what you said."

Bascom smiled, offered his hand again and said, "Matt, we guitar nuts have to stick together."

Man, I really feel like Matt Cale right now, whoever he might be.

Decatur, GA

Matt was surprised how easy the drive down I-75 was until he was about an hour outside of Atlanta. In a span of ten minutes his speed had dropped from seventy miles an hour to under forty. The traffic filled all four lanes and it wasn't even rush hour. *I'm sure not in Buffalo anymore.* He remembered his cousin Dan telling him about the commute times from the suburbs into the downtown, and it sounded to him like there was no close or easy place to live to avoid a long daily drive unless you could live and work right in the center of town. He was used to suburban living and just figured that's what he'd have in Atlanta too, but he knew there would be numerous changes he'd have to face and had resigned himself to dealing with them. His Dad was right, life is portable, even if it did get bogged down in traffic sometimes.

He had printed out Mapquest directions from his laptop back at the hotel, and now he was getting close to the Decatur exit that would take him to Dan's house. It was late morning and Dan was at his office, so Matt was in no hurry to get there. He figured he'd grab lunch somewhere close to Dan's house, drive around to check out an apartment complex that Dan had told him about, and then meet Dan for a beer before they headed back to his house. For the first time since he had left Buffalo, he was feeling totally disconnected; no place to live yet, no job and no local friends. He and Dan were as close as cousins could be but he knew Dan had his own life to live and helping Matt get started would be a complication to him. *The sooner I get settled the* **better, no** *more fun and games for Matt Cale.*

Matt was sitting at the bar at Applebee's when he saw Dan walk in. He waved him over, and their handshake quickly became a guy-hug. "Hey man, you made it," Dan said with a grin.

"Yeah, I made it. That's a whole lot of driving from beautiful Buffalo."

Dan dropped down on the stool next to Matt's and said, "Good timing on your arrival. I was talking about you this morning with a friend of a friend, and he has a lead on a job that's right up your alley."

Matt waited as Dan ordered a glass of white wine, and then replied, "That's good news man, and when did you become a hoity-toity wine drinker?"

Dan grinned. "About a month after I left Buffalo. It happens."

Dan explained the job details to Matt. A friend of his who worked at Georgia Bank knew a man at Venture Group who was looking for someone with a background in mergers and acquisitions. It was a firm that worked with large and very large companies throughout the U.S., Canada and Europe. "I told them a little about you Matt, even though I couldn't answer most of his questions about your background. I just knew you had been working in that kind of stuff for a while and you were hoping to stay in the same arena. That's right, isn't it?"

"Yeah, "Matt answered," it's what I like to do and what I know best." He took a sip of his beer and asked, "So what happens next?"

Dan answered, "Well, I told the guy you'd be calling him one way or another. Can you be ready to meet with Venture Group tomorrow if my friend can arrange it with them?"

"Absolutely, as long as I can get my resume printed someplace."

Dan nodded. "I have a printer at home, and I can even bind it for you if it's more than one page." "It's three pages, and if you can help me with a cover it'll look like I'm a really big deal."

Dan smiled and said, "Yeah, I won't let on that we're both just Buffalo Brats."

Matt followed Dan back to his house and when they got there Dan helped him unpack the Explorer just enough to get to the things he'd need for a few days. Matt picked out a gray suit and a tie for the interview and they carried the rest of his things into the spare bedroom. He went back out to get his guitars and when he got back inside he leaned the cases against the wall of the bedroom.

"You still playing those?" Dan asked.

"Not really, not since I was young and crazy but I'm a businessman now." *I'm gonna miss being Matt Cale.*

While Matt got things squared away in his new temporary home Dan made what passed for a bachelor's evening meal: pasta with marinara sauce from a jar, a salad from bagged greens and a loaf of Italian bread. It was Matt's first non-restaurant meal in days and he was glad to be with a familiar face again. "Finally," he thought, "Things are going to be some kind of normal at last."

Atlanta, GA

It was nearly three o'clock when Matt walked into the lobby of the downtown building where Venture Group was located. It had taken the entire morning for Dan to call his friend, for his friend to call his friend at Venture and then for the interview okay to pass back to Matt. It was more than a little overwhelming to him. He'd been in Atlanta for less than twenty-four hours and was already on his way to a job interview. His financial cushion of $16,455.00 was meant to keep him afloat through what he expected would be a long job search. If things went well with Venture, maybe he wouldn't need to tap into it as much as he had expected.

Venture Group's offices were located in a very tall and very luxurious building in the heart of the downtown business district. Matt walked through the tall bronze doors, signed in at the security desk and walked to the elevator. Venture Group occupied the top two floors of the building and he figured they must have very deep pockets to pay the kind of rent required in a place like this. He got into the elevator with a throng of people, most of who were dressed in trendy urban business attire, and as he looked down at his four year old suit and less than shiny black shoes, he wondered if his Buffalo roots were showing. Finally, he got off on the thirty-first floor and walked straight to the receptionist desk. Expensive looking art lined the walls and the furniture looked like it came from a gallery. When he told the receptionist he was there for an interview with Mr. Hightower, she asked him to take a seat in the large waiting area to her left. He sat down and slowly paged through his resume hoping that his six years at Investar would be enough to impress Hightower. A half-hour long internet search on Venture Group's background earlier that morning left Matt feeling somewhat under-qualified. The company was very big and very successful, and Matt figured they only hired the best of the best.

A small, slender woman in a dark blue pantsuit walked over to him. "Mr. Bingham?"

Matt stood up, smiled and said, "Yes, I'm Matt Bingham."

"Mr. Bingham, please come with me." She walked in front of him down a long, mahogany-paneled corridor and then into a large, plush corner office. "Mr. Hightower is finishing up a meeting and would like you to wait here in his office. He'll only be a moment."

"Sure, that's fine, thank you."

"Would you like any coffee or maybe some bottled water?"

"No thank you, I'm good."

"Please have a seat right here and I'll make sure Mr. Hightower knows you're waiting."

He sat down in one of two large, leather chairs in front of Hightower's desk and looked around the large office. "Wow, this guy has it good," he thought to himself, "an incredible view of downtown, beautiful art and enough space for someone to live in." He looked at the memorabilia on Hightower's credenza and bookcase, and when he saw one particular photograph he froze. It was a picture of a man, a woman and two kids smiling as they stood on a beach. Matt immediately recognized the man in the picture. It was John Higgins. There was no mistaking the dark hair and chiseled good looks. ***Holy shit, what's going on here? Is Hightower John Higgins? He*** stared at the photograph. ***This can't just be a coincidence.*** He studied the photograph more closely and noticed the same, expensive looking watch. The woman standing next to the man was attractive, but not the slim, young and gorgeous Elizabeth that was at the bar with Higgins. His surprise at John Higgins's apparent real identity suddenly gave way to a sickening realization. ***Geez, Higgins . . . or Hightower thinks he met a guy named Matt Cale, a musician. What is he going to think when he finds out I'm really Matt Bingham? I fucking lied to this guy.***

Before he could begin to collect his thoughts and figure things out he heard a voice behind him.

"Sorry to keep you waiting Mr. Bingham."

Matt turned to his right and stood up, looking straight into Hightower's eyes. The look on Hightower's face was one of confusion, then, very slowly, it changed to recognition. ***Shit, he knows.***

"Well, there seems to be a problem here," Hightower said calmly. Matt was feeling anything but calm. "I thought I was here to meet a Matt Bingham who is looking for a job in acquisitions." Matt wasn't sure if it was his role to say something next but Hightower beat him to it. "It looks like someone else is here. It's Mr. Cale, am I right?"

Geez, I am so screwed. "No, it's Bingham. I'm Matt Bingham, just like it says on the resume."

"Well then, I wonder how I got the idea your name was Cale. Any thoughts?" he asked as he sat down in his large, throne-like leather chair.

Jesus, no matter what I say, this is not going to go well. Matt studied Hightower's face for some kind of sign as to what his mood or attitude might be, but couldn't pick up the slightest hint. ***Okay, there's no point in pretending, he knows I gave him a line of shit at the bar.*** He quickly decided that the best defense was a good offense, even though this thing probably wasn't going to end on a happy note. He could just give up now and leave or make an attempt to salvage whatever slim chance he might still have. "You know it's kind of funny," he said, looking over Hightower's shoulder, "When I came in and saw that picture on your credenza, I thought to myself, that man looks just like a guy I met on my way down here, a man named John Higgins." Matt noticed a slight change in Hightower's confident expression as he continued, "But the woman in that picture wasn't the woman who was with him at the bar, so of course I just figured I must be wrong." He looked directly into Hightower's eyes, looking for a sign that the guy might pull back a little. Hightower sat very still, looking at Matt as if he was sizing him up. ***What in the hell is this, a competition?***

Finally, Hightower said, "That's my wife Melanie. She's also my business partner. We were on vacation in the Bahamas."

Matt replied, "Never been there myself. I hear a lot of the people there have British accents." *Let's see what that brings.*

Hightower leaned back in his chair, looking at the ceiling, and then lowered his gaze toward Matt. "Your resume is very solid, good background in acquisitions." For a moment it sounded like he wanted to change the subject, but then he shifted gears again. "But it didn't say much about who you are as a person, like whether you had any hobbies or talents, like maybe music. One would think that a person with that kind of talent would want to make sure people knew it."

Geez, could you be any more obvious? Matt tried to act cordial and remain under control but it was getting harder to pretend there wasn't something going on here. *This guy is so slick, what is he looking for here?* "Well, actually, I used to play guitar in a band back home and I'm still pretty good at it when I take the time."

Hightower stroked his chin and said, "I have a friend, his name is Alan and he's really talented. All he talks about is getting into the music business and he just reminded me yesterday that he expects me to help him out somehow."

Why is he telling me something he knows he already told me? "Well," Matt replied, "tell him everyone has to pay his dues before he can find success."

"Yes, I understand that and I agree," Hightower replied, "but it never hurts to get a little help from someone who says he's in the business and knows people."

Okay, he's calling me out. "You're right, that's the best kind of help, even though it usually comes at a price." *Will he get my hint?*

Matt couldn't tell for sure, but it seemed like Hightower was starting to show signs of nervousness about the conversation they were having. When Matt said the word "price" he could see the change in Hightower's expression. *Let's try a different approach here.* "I spent some time looking at your website," Matt started, "and you really seem to be on a roll lately with some great acquisitions. Your clients must be very happy."

Hightower made a very slight nod but didn't seem to want to change the subject. *He's really, really nervous about something.*

Hightower stated, "I really need to do whatever it takes to help Alan, maybe you have some ideas on how we can help each other here."

Why is he so obsessed with talking about his friend Alan, this is supposed to be a job interview? It's almost like he's afraid of what will happen if he lets Alan down on the music thing.

Matt was really torn about what to do. He had driven all the way from Buffalo to start a new life. He was a newcomer to Atlanta and needed a job, a job in his chosen field so he wouldn't have to start all over doing something else and just giving up the years of opportunity he had worked so hard to earn. And here he was interviewing with a guy who obviously lacked the integrity and morals to simply live a decent, honest life. The uncomfortable silence between the two of them seemed to bother both men. Hightower turned to his credenza and poured himself a glass of ice water without offering any to Matt. Matt flipped mindlessly through the copy of his resume in his lap. It was when he glanced at another photograph on Hightower's desk that something finally dawned on him. It was a picture of Hightower's wedding. A large group of elegant people, in an elegant setting, with a very spontaneous posing of the groom's family on one side and the bride's on the other. And there, standing beside Melanie was a young man holding a guitar with one hand, his other arm around her, and he was smiling and looking over at John Hightower. *I'll bet that's Alan.*

Matt thought to himself, "This conversation is going nowhere and I need to do something one way or another." He cleared his throat and said, "That's a great wedding photo. "Who's the guy with the guitar standing next to your wife?"

Hightower turned and looked directly at Matt, his surprise and nervousness showing on his face. "Well, as a matter of fact, that's her brother." He paused a moment, the continued, "Her brother is the Alan I told you about who's looking for a break in the music business."

Okay, I got it now. Alan knows about sweet, young Elizabeth and Hightower needs to kiss his ass and get him some kind of showbiz connection to shut **him up.** Matt hesitated a moment before saying anything. What could he say? What should he say that would help his situation? He was interviewing for a job with a man who was a bullshit artist, who he had met by being a bullshit artist himself. Hightower could have just told Matt the interview was over the moment they recognized each other. That would get Matt out of the picture but it wouldn't help Hightower's situation with Alan, and it was obvious that was very important to him. *Geez, maybe its time for Matt Cale to help out his friend Matt Bingham.*

Matt leaned back and crossed his legs, making sure Hightower got the hint that he was comfortable, unflappable and interested in continuing their discussion. He looked directly at Hightower. "We seem to be having two separate conversations here," he said.

Hightower nodded in agreement. "Yes, we are, but in a way they just might come down to the same thing."

Okay, he's trying to make a point here, and it's up to him to make it. Matt nodded but sat silently, waiting for Hightower to continue his thought.

"It looks like we both need something here," Hightower began. "I know from my end exactly what I can deliver, but I'm not sure if you really have any skin in the game."

Okay, he wants to know if I can help him get out from under Alan. "By that you mean you don't think I really have any contacts in the music business."

"Well, I'm having trouble understanding how an Acquisitions Specialist from Buffalo, New York is connected to anyone in Nashville, Los Angeles or anywhere else they make music that isn't Buffalo."

Okay, how am I going to play this? Matt uncrossed and then re-crossed his legs, still looking straight at Hightower. "Well, it just so happens that I know an agent in Nashville. He's a talent agent and he books acts, mostly newcomers."

Hightower looked at Matt with a smirk. "Do you know this man as well as you know Dierks Bentley and the other stars you talked about at the bar?"

Okay, score one for Hightower. After a few seconds where neither man spoke, Matt cleared his throat and said, "A second ago you mentioned you had something you could deliver." Hightower nodded but said nothing. *Geez, this has turned into liars—poker, or more like liars-chess.*

Hightower finally replied, "And I said I didn't think you had any skin in this game. Is this supposed agent friend of yours intended to be your answer to our little problem here?"

Matt answered, "It might be, if we can stop dancing and get to some kind of point."

Hightower looked at him and smiled. "You sure have balls Bingham, I'll give you that."

Matt replied, "It takes balls, really big ones, to be good in the acquisition world." Hightower's smile didn't fade, and he nodded in agreement. *Wow, did I actually impress this guy?*

Matt gestured toward the photograph behind Hightower's desk. "So tell me, how good is Alan on that guitar?"

Hightower turned just long enough to glance at the wedding picture and replied, "I don't know how to answer that. I told you at the bar that night that he was very talented but I have no idea if that's true. He seemed to be pretty good playing at a wedding reception, but to be honest, everyone was drunk."

"To be honest", that's an interesting choice of words. Matt smiled. "Understood," he said. "The reason I asked is that my agent friend is really a guitar man. He wants guys who can play their ass off all night long. Is that Alan?"

"I don't know, I suppose he can," Hightower said, his frustration clear in his tone. "But let's get something straight. All I promised the little pecker was an introduction, not a guarantee or a contract. All I need is for your friend to meet him, listen to him play for a few minutes and then decide if the kid is any good. To be perfectly honest, I don't give a rat's ass if he gets a contract or not. My debt will be paid."

Again with the perfectly honest stuff. Geez, what a warm, fuzzy guy. Matt nodded his understanding. "Okay, so now I have an angle on how to solve your problem, but how do we solve mine?"

"By that you mean a job with this firm?"

"Exactly, after all, that's why I'm here today."

Hightower leaned forward, his forearms resting on his desk. He looked straight into Matt's eyes and said, "Okay, the job is yours on the condition that you set something up between Alan and this agent friend of yours, and you have to make sure that Alan knows the referral came from me."

Matt nodded his understanding, paused, then replied, "And I assume that Venture Group will put this into some type of employment contract."

Hightower looked offended as he sat up ramrod straight in his chair and, as if spitting the words, he said, "Mr. Bingham, you don't need a contract, you have my word on it."

It seemed to Matt that there wasn't much more to say. He took a breath, stood up and extended his hand toward Hightower. "Thanks for your time, sir, if it's okay with you I'll get back to you in the morning." Their handshake was quick and insincere. During the ride down in the elevator and in his car on the way back to Dan's house he kept hearing the same phrase over and over in his head. "You have my word on it." By the time he pulled into the driveway he was smiling.

Nashville, TN

Rupert Bascom leaned forward in his desk chair, digging through the bottom file drawer of his desk as he struggled to keep his phone nestled in the crook of his neck. "And you're sure about those dates in April, the ones for the Basement," he said to the person at the other end of the call. He pulled out a manila folder and spread the contents across his desk. The person on the phone seemed to drone on and on, and finally Bascom interrupted, "Look, we need to get that firmed up. You heard the MP3 I sent you and I heard this guy play everything from ballads to roadhouse. I'm telling you, if you don't grab him right now I've got at least three other bands that will." After a brief reply from the other end, Bascom nodded and said, "Great, he's here right now. I'll get the paperwork pulled together by the end of the day and drop it off at your place on my way home tonight."

He hung up the phone and leaned back in his chair, shaking his head. "My God, that guy can talk the whole goddamned day and never say a thing." He pulled a stack of legal-looking forms from the papers he had spread out, turned them around to face the front of the desk, and said, "Okay Matt, it took a few promises from me but from what that guy just told me it looks like I found you a band that needs your guitar. Are you sure it's what you want, and have I made things clear on what this is and what you can expect?"

Matt smiled broadly and answered, "Absolutely man, I'm ready."

Before Matt could finish reading through all of the forms and contract language Bascom said, "Oh, by the way, when we were sitting at the bar that night you mentioned you knew a guy, a good guitar guy. Do you still think I should talk to him?"

Matt looked up from his reading, laughed and said, "Oh, you mean Alan, uh, no . . . no, I don't think so. I heard he's in the middle of some big family problems."

"WAY NORTH OF LUCKY"

1

The article in Sunday's *Arizona Republic* seemed to be an island of good news in a sea of economic negativity. Nathan Haas sat at his kitchen counter, staring at the headline: *Troubled Downtown Development Finally Underway.* His boss had told him that the article would be on the front page of the business section, but until he actually saw it he had refused to celebrate. He had been working for over a year on the deal for his client to acquire the half-built *Esperanza* project; an ambitious mixed-use revival of an historic Mexican barrio on the edge of the main downtown business district. A succession of three teams of national and local developers had tried to keep the project afloat after the recession began, but one by one they were forced to sell the project for less than they paid for it.

Nathan sipped his morning coffee and read the article slowly, pouring through the list of names of people who had tried and failed to make a go of a promising concept but couldn't seem to make it to the finish line. Despite the reputations and experience of the development teams, nothing worked. It was as though the project was cursed. His world of commercial real estate was one of numbers, statistics, projections and pragmatism. The fact that three good, strong teams had all tried and failed seemed to lead to the idea that simple bad luck was involved. When an acquaintance at Desert Horizons Development approached him about the project, all he could think was "Do I really want to be involved with loser number four on this thing?"

After his conversation with Desert Horizons, he had gone to his boss, Greg DeGeorge, to discuss going ahead with the project. Greg reminded him that the office slogan "Hand it to Haas" came about because of Nathan's uncanny ability to turn bad luck into good. So many times other brokers in the office couldn't close their deals despite doing everything right. Nathan would be handed the situation and, as if fortune shined down upon him, things got done and the deal got closed. Unfortunately it sometimes meant another broker got cut out of the deal or lost his job but Nathan just figured that was part of the risk of being in their line of work. While he enjoyed the recognition of having some kind of gift in business dealings, he couldn't help but think that he was just plain lucky. Like the timing was right or the stars were aligned or there was just good juju on his side. He never really considered himself to be a gifted deal-maker. He just felt lucky.

He got up, walked over to the coffeemaker and refilled his cup then sat back down at the counter. The newspaper article included a full-color architect's rendering of the main entrance gates to the project and what the development would look like when it was completed. Below the rendering was a picture of Nathan. "Geez, I look older than 42," he thought to himself. The black and white photo made his sandy colored hair look gray and his tan wasn't apparent. "Time to get a new headshot taken," he thought as he resumed reading. He was named as the lead broker for Sonoran Properties and was quoted several times in the article along with the Mayor and the president of Desert Horizons. It was a bit of an ego boost and he tossed the section of newspaper on to the counter. "I'll put it in an envelope and send it to mom and dad tomorrow", he thought as he headed for the shower. He wondered if anyone at his office saw the article.

The Monday drive on SR-51 was the usual slow and go commute to the downtown. About a mile after he entered the highway a large diesel pick-up truck loaded with construction debris entered the road and traveled in the right lane. He noticed that the pile of junk looked like it wasn't properly strapped down and bits and pieces of gypsum board were falling on to the pavement and the truck driver signaled that he was moving over into his lane. He looked to his left and saw the car beside him accelerate enough to give him room to move over. He was no sooner in that lane when what seemed like the entire load of debris in the pick-up broke loose. Luckily he was able to avoid it by moving left on to the shoulder of the road, but he could see in his rear view mirror that the driver behind him wasn't so lucky and couldn't avoid driving right into the middle of the flying debris. The driver swerved to get out from behind the pick-up and ended up side-swiping a minivan. Nathan drove on down the road and he could see in his mirror that about a dozen drivers were braking hard and swerving to avoid the dangerous mix of lumber, glass and bricks. "Holy shit," he muttered, "I dodged a bullet on that one."

Maria, the receptionist and office mother hen was waiting when Nathan walked into the lobby. "Congratulations Mr. Haas," she said, grinning and rushing from behind her desk to hug him. Maria was as wide as she was tall and a hug from her was a full body experience.

He smiled and replied, "Thanks Maria, no big deal."

"Bullshit, it's a hell of a big deal," his friend James called out.

Nathan had barely gotten loose from Maria's ample frame when his friend James's long arms enveloped him in a bear hug. James was a former college and pro basketball player and even though Nathan was an even six feet tall, James' hug made him feel small.

"Damn, that was a great article," James bellowed. "You got it done, my man!"

Nathan was finally able to pull away when James eased up on his hug. "I appreciate your enthusiasm," Nathan answered, feeling embarrassed, "but I think I was just in the right place at the right time."

Greg DeGeorge was just entering the lobby and said, "It was a hell of a lot more than timing. You have some kind of magic going, you're a machine."

The attention was flattering and Nathan reminded himself not to take it too seriously. He honestly didn't feel that he had done anything that the other team's brokers hadn't done. He couldn't explain his success as anything but luck, and he intended to keep it in perspective. He also knew that the original broker on the deal, who had tried and failed three times, was probably going to lose his job. That took some of the shine off this spontaneous little celebration.

He spent the bulk of his workday trying to focus on a new opportunity. Greg had suggested that a second potential deal, the *Mesa Norte* resort project might be handed to him because another broker in the office, Nick Porreco, was having trouble with the client. Nathan detested Porreco, a slimy, grinning, muscle-bound jerk. He was a lounge lizard type of guy who thought charm and bullshit were the only tools required to close a deal. In the two years they had worked together Nathan had been lucky enough to avoid teaming with the man, but it looked like that streak was about to end. He had planned to take Greg aside and request that he work on the deal alone rather than teaming with Porreco. He knew he could handle the deal on his own but Greg was always reluctant to take a client away from one of his brokers under any circumstances.

At 2:30 PM he went down to the coffee bar in the main building lobby for his regular mid-afternoon caffeine pick-me-up. As he got off the elevator back up on his office floor, a young woman came rushing toward him and called out, "Hold the door please!"

He reached back just in time to keep the doors from closing and held them until the woman got inside.

"Thanks," she said with a grateful smile.

He nodded, smiled back at her and walked down the corridor to his office. For the rest of the day he buried himself in the Mesa Norte files, trying to absorb the history of the project and trying to understand why Porreco couldn't seem to close the deal.

At 5:20 he packed up his briefcase, shut off his office lights and headed for the elevator. When he got there a small group of people were gathered near Maria's desk and he saw a bright orange safety cone on the floor in front of the elevator. "What's going on Dave?" he asked a short, balding man at the edge of the crowd.

"Didn't you hear?" the man replied. "Amy from accounting is trapped in the elevator. She's been stuck in there since like 2:30. They have a repair crew working on it"

"Holy shit," Nathan said, "I was on it right before she got on. I even held the door for her."

"Well, consider yourself lucky, man, because that could have been you in there."

Nathan thought about how close he came to being the one trapped because the elevator obviously failed just seconds after he got off it. He hesitated a moment, looking around at the people waiting by the desk, and finally realized there was nothing he could do to help the poor woman. He opened the door to the stairwell and hurried out of the building.

2

Nathan was sitting at his patio table, looking through his mail and trying to finish reading the morning newspaper when he heard a soft, female voice from behind.

"Hi honey, I thought I'd find you out here." He smiled and stood up just as Brooke reached his side. They kissed and Brooke dropped into a chair across from him. "I can't stay too long, I was just picking up a few things for dinner and thought I'd stop by to congratulate you on the newspaper article."

Nathan looked at her and, as usual, was struck by her quiet beauty. She was petite, fresh looking without the need for a lot of make-up and, he thought, was the perfect combination of country and big city. They had been dating off and on for eighteen months and had recently gotten back together after two months of a break to see if their relationship had a chance for permanence. He was still gun-shy about marriage after his divorce, even though people told him he was lucky to get through so quickly and painlessly. Brooke had gone through her own marital split and seemed to be handling it very well, but that was typical of the way she viewed life. One of the many things he loved about her was her gentle sense of harmony with everything around her, and her belief that there is a reason for everything and there was a natural rhythm to life. Brooke was very much a yin and yang person. It seemed a perfect match with her calm demeanor and her soft, natural look.

"So are we still on for Saturday at my place?" Brooke asked.

He nodded, "Absolutely, what can I bring?"

"Just bring some wine, I have dinner covered, and I'll pick up dessert somewhere."

He gathered up the pile of mail, arranged it into a neat stack and then turned back to Brooke. She was looking at him with a slight, awkward smile. "What?" he asked, jokingly suspicious.

Brooke's smile widened. "Oh I was just thinking about a conversation we had a few months ago. Remember, we talked about balance, about how everything in life needs its counterpoint to be fully appreciated?"

"Yeah," he replied, "You reminded me that everything has an upside and a downside, a good and a bad."

Brooke's smile didn't change. "Honey," she said, "I look at you and see someone who seems unusually blessed with good fortune. I hope you take the time to appreciate it once in a while."

Nathan smiled and nodded his acknowledgement. He knew very well that he had experienced very little pain or unpleasantness in his life. He'd enjoyed a happy, stable childhood, four years of college that brought him several job offers and a totally normal life since then. Since his divorce two years before, his life was rolling along smoothly, even though his ex-wife had fallen on hard times. He looked at Brooke again. "What brought on the good fortune remark?" he asked.

"Oh I'm so proud of you for the article in the paper and for all you've got going on in your life. I just want you to take time to enjoy the good karma that's around you."

Nathan nodded in agreement, then smiled and said, "The karma thing again." Brooke just smiled and rolled her eyes.

They talked for a few more minutes, then Brooke stood up and he walked her to the front door. "See you Saturday," she said softly and kissed him. They lingered in the kiss longer than usual but finally Brooke broke away and left through the open door. He stood there watching her get into her car. He knew their relationship couldn't hang indefinitely in limbo, but he wasn't sure where it was going. They were in love but for some reason they were unable to get things out of neutral.

The next day Nathan's office was still buzzing about Amy, the woman who had been trapped in the elevator. It had taken the rescue crew until eight o'clock in the evening to free her and she was understandably distraught over the ordeal. Nathan thought again of how close he had come to being the one trapped. He considered contacting Amy but quickly decided against it. He was certain that, sitting alone for hours in a dark elevator, she must have thought about how he had just gotten out of the ill-fated cab and held the door for her to enter it. It was normal for people to feel like they had been in the wrong place at the wrong time and that it could have or should have happened to someone else. There was no sense reminding her that it could just as easily been him that became trapped.

He had no sooner sat down at his desk and turned on his computer when Nick Porreco walked in.

"Hey dude," Nick said as he dropped into a chair in front of Nathan's desk.

Nathan's first thought was that Porreco looked even tanner than his normal, year-round tanning bed look, and that his hair was dyed even blacker than usual. An Italian man in his late 40s without the slightest hint of gray hair was definitely spending extra time at his hair salon. "Morning, Nick," Nathan replied, struggling to be friendly.

Porreco leaned forward in the chair, "Greg just informed that he wants you to take the lead on Mesa Norte."

"Yeah," Nathan answered, "I knew he was thinking in that direction."

"Well," Nick replied, "I told him I didn't like his decision. It's my deal and my client and I don't need anybody's help."

Nathan wanted to just say something like, "You have totally fucked up this whole thing and it was the client who told Greg to find someone to fix it." But, instead, he paused to choose his words carefully. "It doesn't matter who's in on the negotiations, the important thing is that we win it." He looked at Porreco's expression, and his normal Cheshire Cat grin was gone.

"I've spent two years on this deal and now I have to split it with you. How is that fair?"

Nathan sighed and answered, "That's a conversation between you and Greg. In the meantime I have a few ideas and the whole Mesa Norte team will be here tomorrow to discuss them."

Porreco's face turned red and he asked, "Were you planning to fill me in on things or just leave me hanging?"

Nathan knew that sooner or later the conversation would become contentious. Porreco was arrogant and controlling and no one in the office liked working with him. Before answering him, Nathan turned to his computer, typed out a brief message, clicked *Send* and leaned back in his chair. "Okay, I just sent you my plan and a matrix that shows the original numbers and my ideas on where they need to be. There's also an edited version of our piece of the marketing plan." Nathan knew his ideas weren't drastically different from the original ones, but he knew he could make them sound better.

Porreco glared. "Sounds like you have everything going your way, just like *Esperanza.*"

"Well," Nathan replied, "I don't think it should be referred to as *my way* but I think it's something the client will buy into." Porreco stood up, his face still red, and walked out of the room. "Geez," Nathan thought, "why does Greg keep that asshole on the payroll?"

Nathan knew the meeting with the Mesa Norte team would not be brief or easy. There was a lot of anger and a lot of bruised egos among the group, and he had been thrust smack into the middle of it. There were two developers, three banks, a land planner, architect, civil engineer and a national marketing firm involved and he had a hunch that Porreco had pissed off all or most of them. As the parties trickled one by one into the room Nathan did his best to be warm and cordial. The tension in the air was palpable. Porreco walked in and took his customary seat in the middle chair of the huge conference table. Greg had made it clear that Nathan was to be in charge of the meeting but it was obvious Porreco wasn't going to give him an inch of ground.

When everyone had arrived and gotten their coffee and beverages, Nathan looked around the room at the sea of gray, khaki and navy blue. Even the women were attired in their best corporate colors. He thanked them all for coming on such short notice and expressed his appreciation for their patience. Porreco started to interrupt him but was quickly cut off by Sherman Heddrick, the lead developer.

"Mr. Haas," he said firmly, "it's our understanding that you have taken over the effort for your firm, and we'd like to hear what you have to say. Hopefully it will be different than what we have heard so far."

Nathan wanted to throw a big grin at Porreco but maintained his control and said, "Thanks, Sherman, I think you'll like what we've put together."

For the next two hours Nathan mapped out his ideas and listened to feedback from the group. There were numerous side conversations and he had to work hard to maintain order. Gradually the mood in the room shifted from tension to conciliation. When it became clear that the development team was in favor of the new plan, Porreco stood up and left the room without saying a single word. Finally Heddrick said, "Well, at long last it looks like this thing is going to work." He stood, reached across the table and shook Nathan's hand.

Nathan smiled and replied, "I'm glad you agree, Sherman, we're ready to make it happen."

Word of the Mesa Norte success spread quickly through the office. Nathan was just hanging up his phone after a call to Brooke to tell her the good news when Greg walked in.

He looked at Nathan, spread his arms wide, and bellowed "Hand it to Haas!"

Nathan grinned and said, "Yeah, well, it worked out pretty damned well after all."

"Great job, Nathan, great job, you're on a real winning streak these days."

Nathan nodded, somewhat embarrassed at Greg's praise. "I guess when you get lucky you stay lucky."

Greg said, "Call it luck or whatever you want, but you sure seem to have a ton of it."

"Thanks Greg," he replied, hoping the conversation would change.

Greg turned around, reached back and slowly closed the door. "I thought I should fill you in on a decision I just made," he said quietly. "I'm going to tell Nick Porreco he's through here." Nathan wasn't sure of what the proper reaction to the news should be. On the one hand he was very glad that Porreco would finally be gone, but on the other hand a man was about to lose his job in a bad economy and in a strange way he felt responsible.

"Well, I guess that's your call to make Greg," he said, trying to appear detached and unemotional.

Greg nodded and said, "I take full responsibility for him, he was a bad hire and I should have been paying more attention to what was going on."

"Well, do what you have to do and let me know if I can fill in the blanks on Mesa Norte," Nathan said.

Greg nodded, shrugged and opened the door. "Again, great job, and I'm glad I handed it to Haas." he said as he walked out. Greg had no sooner left when James walked in.

"Hey, big guy," Nathan said with a smile.

James seemed to fill the entire doorway as he stood there grinning. After a knee injury ended his brief basketball career he went into the real estate field. He had joined Sonoran Properties the same year as Nathan and the two had become close friends. "Shit man, you did it again! How about lettin' some of that good juju rub off on me." He sat down in the chair in front of the desk, his long legs splayed out in front of him.

Nathan smiled broadly. Whenever James was around there seemed to be fun in the air. The man had a constant broad smile, an infectious, upbeat attitude and a sense of humor that was never far from the surface. Nathan replied, "My juju is available by prescription only, consult your physician."

James let out his usual cackling laugh. "Okay man, I'll do that."

"Hey man, reach back and close the door," Nathan said quietly. He opened the bottom drawer of his desk and pulled out a half-empty bottle of bourbon. He found two slightly used Styrofoam cups in the drawer and said, "Christmas party leftovers."

James grinned, looked at his watch and said, "Hell, it's five o'clock somewhere."

As they sipped the bourbon, Nathan handed James a copy of the financial matrix and marketing changes and said, "It really wasn't vastly different from the deal Porreco showed them."

James looked up from reading the matrix and said, "Yeah, I heard Greg is thinking of brooming that mother fucker, and good riddance."

Nathan knew he could be totally open with James and didn't try to hide his pleasure. "Now Nick can take his fake smile and dyed hair and pursue a lucrative career in the used car industry."

They both laughed, lifted their cups in a mock toast to Porreco, and launched into a fifteen minute exchange of sarcastic stories about the man's numerous flirtations with the female employees and his constant bragging about his sexual conquests. As funny as the stories seemed to some of the guys in the office, there was a sad and pathetic tone to them as well.

Finally, James stood up, stretching his long frame, handed his empty cup to Nathan and said, "Well all I can say is this company is lucky to have you man."

Nathan smiled and looked down at his desk, "Well, I have to say I'm the lucky one." As James left the room Nathan felt the same, strange sense of good fortune that he felt when the Esperanza deal wrapped up. It seemed as though luck had shined down on him once more.

3

Dinner with Brooke was relaxing and stimulating at the same time. They had slowly and steadily built a good relationship, a balance of affection, passion and trust. And along with it came a very strong intellectual bond. Nathan's love of art, music and the creative process was a perfect mix with Brooke's deep interest in Eastern philosophies and spirituality. Their relationship had included numerous hours-long conversations on the forces that effect thinking and events in the world. Nathan was a staunch atheist but he enjoyed listening to Brooke read to him from her books on Taoism and Buddhist concepts. She believed strongly that there was a balance in the universe that translated to a balance in every person's life.

Nathan stood to begin clearing the table, his usual contribution to their dinner activities. Brooke was very talented in the kitchen and he was an efficient clean-up man. "Another part of her balanced universe", he had thought numerous times. "Want another glass of wine while I clean up?" he asked.

"Sure, she said, brushing her long dark hair back from her face and holding out her glass for him. He poured the last bit of Pinot Noir and said, "Finish that and I'll open another bottle when I get the dishwasher loaded." Brooke sat on a stool at the kitchen island as Nathan went through his routine of scrape, rinse and load. They talked about the previous day's dust storm that had blown through the northeast part of town, and how he had watched through his kitchen window as a small funnel of a dust devil luckily missed the tree in his front yard and touched down on his next door neighbor's garage, sending roof tiles flying in every direction. Brooke told him about a meeting she had scheduled with a City Councilman to discuss a marketing plan for a new solar energy initiative, and how the guy was being evasive with his backing of the plan. Their professional lives were hectic but rewarding, and their personal life was still a work in progress. Finally, when Nathan was finished with the kitchen chores he opened a bottle of wine and they walked out to the patio.

"So honey," Brooke began, "tell me the rest of the Mesa Norte story. Did Nick leave yet?"

Nathan took a sip from his glass and said, "Yeah, yesterday was his last day. He sure wasn't his usual overbearing asshole self, that's for sure."

Brooke nodded. "Well I can understand that. He's out of work in this damned economy and I'm guessing Greg won't be giving him a good reference to use looking for a new job."

Nathan answered, "I have no idea what Greg said to him but I'm sure it wasn't pleasant on either side of the desk." Brooke was looking at him with the same curious smile he often saw on her face. "Okay, what are you thinking?" he asked. "Are you thinking how good fortune has shined down on me again?"

Brooke nodded. "I know from all the stories you told me that Nick was a total asshole and I'm sure he screwed things up with the deal, but it still took you to save the day."

Nathan was still uncomfortable with his new role of *Office Magician* and continued his belief that he was simply on a lucky streak. "I told Greg and James and everyone else that I'm a very lucky guy and not some deal making genius, let's just call it what it is."

Brooke looked straight into his eyes and said, "I've been thinking about you a lot lately, even more than usual."

He had heard that before and answered, "Yeah I know babe, me too. I don't know where all this is going between us either."

Brooke's eyebrows rose slightly and she said, "Whoa big fella, I'm not talking about that." Her tone seemed almost defensive but the softness in her eyes kept the mood at a comfortable level. "What I mean is, I've been thinking about all of the good fortune, the good things that are happening to you or as you like to call it, your good luck." He looked at her, sensing that she had a lot more to say on the subject. "I know you don't always agree with me on my Taoist ideas, I mean about how seemingly contrary forces are interconnected and interdependent in the world."

Nathan waited to make sure she was finished, and then said, "You mean your yin and yang thing."

Brooke nodded and said, "It's not a thing, honey, it's a belief system that makes sense and brings order to our lives."

He softened his tone. "I'm sorry, babe, I'm not making light of things here."

Brooke seemed reassured and continued. "Honey, the events in your life lately are what have made me think about you so much. It seems like the stasis between the opposing fortunes and actions in your life is out of balance."

Nathan sat there, took another sip of wine and looked at Brooke, her beautiful blue eyes focused intently on him.

He paused, trying to choose his words very carefully and to understand what Brooke was trying to say. "Okay babe, if I'm reading you right, here is what I heard. You think I'm too lucky. You believe in such a true and total balance, so all of my good luck must mean that someone else is having just as much bad luck."

Brooke answered so quickly she almost stepped on his final words. "All I'm saying is the fact you are so consistently and incredibly lucky seems to suggest an imbalance."

Nathan wanted her to know he was trying hard to understand her point in the whole discussion but he was more than a little confused. "Is this imbalance on a personal scale, like just in my life or does it affect other people? I mean, am I fucking up other people's lives?" His words were no sooner out of his mouth when they sounded patronizing and sarcastic. "Wait babe, that didn't come out right," he said quickly. "You've told me so many times how there is personal balance, relationship balance and world balance. I'm just trying to understand what you mean when you say my good luck has led to some kind of imbalance."

Brooke leaned back in her chair and sat cross-legged, her aqua blouse, red painted toenails and the lemon colored chair cushion creating a colorful backdrop to the conversation. She took a sip of wine and looked out at her cactus garden, then said, "I'm not really sure, it's not like I'm some mystical expert on things. I just believe that when one person seems to have an over-abundance of good fortune, someone, somewhere is suffering from a lack of it."

"Geez," Nathan replied, "that almost makes me feel guilty."

Brooke showed a faint smile but didn't respond. A moment later she said, "I'm not asking you to think about your entire life, just think about this past month or two. There was the big closing you had last month and that near-miss with all that construction junk on the 51. I saw in the paper that seven cars were damaged in that mess. There was the woman in the elevator and the two real estate deals that cost two people their jobs. And the dust devil that decided to leave you alone and hit your neighbor instead. Doesn't all of that make you wonder what's going on?"

Nathan was feeling increasingly uncomfortable with the conversation. He felt like he'd been riding a wave of good luck and now it seemed like Brooke wanted to find something bad in the situation. He answered her calmly, "Look babe, I really haven't thought too deeply about any of this. I'm just enjoying the way things are going. I thought you wanted me to appreciate it."

"I do, honey," she replied, "of course I do. But I also want you to be aware of how the people in your life, or someone you don't even know might be affected by the things that happen to you, or the things that don't happen."

Nathan sat in his chair, holding his wine glass close to his lips but not drinking. Brooke continued, "Look, I know you don't really buy into my belief system, what you refer to as my yin and yang thing, but when yin and yang are equally present everything is calm and as it should be."

He sighed and answered, "Okay, that's something we agree on, my life is pretty calm right now. Life is good."

"Yes," Brooke replied, "but only if you look at your own life separate from the rest of the world. We're all in this world together."

Nathan felt his patience wavering. He took a sip of wine, paused and asked, "So what do you suggest? Should I just stay in my house and not go anywhere or do anything so my good luck won't cause bad luck for somebody?"

Brooke didn't like his sarcasm and replied, "Of course not, and you know that's not my point."

"No I don't know that," he snapped, "I have no idea whatsoever what your point is." It might have been the four glasses of wine or it might have been his lack of shared interest in Brooke's Taoist ideas, but something was definitely starting to have an effect on his mood. He tried to be patient, and after a few uncomfortable seconds of silence, he said, "Maybe I should go, this is turning into something I don't want it to turn into."

Brooke nodded her agreement and said, "Just take a few minutes to think about all of this, okay?" Nathan stood up and carried his empty glass into the kitchen. Brooke followed him and as he turned to head for the front door she stepped in front of him and put her arms around his waist. She looked up into his eyes and said, "I'm sorry if it seems like I'm picking a fight, I'm really not. I just want to understand the things that are going on around you, that's all."

"Fair enough," Nathan answered, bending down to kiss her. They held each other for a few moments, kissed again and Nathan opened the door. "I'll call you tomorrow," he said.

4

Sunday morning was the same typical routine Nathan followed every week; out of bed by seven o'clock, iced coffee and the newspaper on the patio then a few hours of yard work and housekeeping. But the mood wasn't quite as relaxing as it usually was. His conversation with Brooke the night before was filling his thoughts. Every time he tried to dismiss her comments about a balance in life he came back to the nagging fact that she was right, and that the constant luck he was having was anything but normal. How many times could he write it off as just a string of coincidences? And his recent lucky streak brought back something that he had thought about his entire life. Very little bad luck had ever come his way. That fact had always been easy to brush off, but now Brooke had made him aware that there was something real about the whole thing. A force of some kind seemed to be at work, guiding and following him. As much as he wanted to laugh it off as Brooke's spiritual ideas or even as pure superstition, there was no denying the unwavering good fortune that filled his life. It was as though he was bulletproof to bad luck.

He made a quick trip down the street to Walgreens to pick up a prescription for his allergies. The parking lot was nearly empty that early on a Sunday morning and he had his pick of parking spaces. He had to wait at the pharmacy counter and while he was killing time browsing in the magazine aisle he heard a commotion at the front of the store. He walked in that direction and saw two employees and several customers gawking out the front door. When he got close enough to look outside he saw that a black pick-up truck had crashed into the side of a minivan and as he got a better look he saw that the minivan was in the parking space beside his Lexus. "Holy shit," he muttered. He walked outside and saw that the truck had impacted the van in a direct line toward the side door, made contact at the center post, and had pushed the van to where it almost touched Nathan's car. "Geez," he thought, "a freakin' T-bone. That could have been my car." The driver of the van was rushing from the store and Nathan stood next to his own car to watch what happened next. The driver of the pick-up, a tall, thin young man with a baseball cap turned backward, was explaining to one of the Walgreens employees that his foot had slipped off the brake pedal and he couldn't stop in time.

Nathan watched, listened, and then walked back into the store. He knew that, if it weren't for the fact the minivan driver chose the parking space next to his he would be the one shouting at the kid in the truck. On the drive back home he thought again about Brooke's comments on his uncommon amount of luck.

When he got home he called Brooke and they agreed to meet at Tres Amigos, their favorite tavern, at three o'clock. He got there about two-thirty so he could have a beer and watch a little bit of the Cardinals game before Brooke arrived. He was no sooner on his stool when the bartender approached with a grin. "Hey Mr. Haas, how the hell are you?" he called out.

"I'm fine Mike, how have you been?"

"Well, since you asked, my hemorrhoids are killin' me and so is my back."

Nathan grinned, "I can always count on you to be honest, I'll give you that."

"Well, don't you get tired of people just saying *fine* when someone asks them how they're doing? At least I'm being straight with you."

Nathan smiled and Mike asked, "The usual?" "Yep, and make it a 20-ounce," Nathan answered.

Mike walked to the taps and slowly filled a frosted mug with the house Pale Ale, then placed it on a coaster in front of Nathan and said, "So I saw the story about you in the paper last week. Nice."

Nathan smiled and said, "It was about the project, not me, but thanks."

Mike glanced down the bar at a man who was trying to get his attention. "Be right back," he said. Nathan watched the Cardinal game for a few minutes then looked down the bar and noticed that Mike was having trouble with the taps. The same keg of ale Nathan had ordered was pouring nothing but creamy white foam. He heard Mike swearing and telling another bartender that he had just loaded in a new keg that morning and it was their last one. As Mike walked back to give the customer the bad news he said to Nathan, "Looks like you got the last Pale Ale, my friend, the keg just crapped out."

Nathan watched a few more minutes of the football game, and then felt hands on his shoulders. As he started to turn Brooke kissed his neck and said, "Hi honey."

He leaned forward and kissed her, then helped her move her barstool closer to his. "Good timing, "he said, "I was ready to order another beer and Mike looks really busy so I'll order yours too." "I'm in the mood for something besides beer," she said, as if she was thinking it over. Finally she said "How about a vodka and tonic?"

"Wow, babe, that's a serious drink for Sunday football."

"Yeah, well I feel like something besides the same ole same ole."

Nathan waved to get Mike's attention and he finally walked toward them." "Hey, beautiful!" he said to Brooke with a leering smile. "You still in love with this guy or are you ready for a change?"

Nathan smiled, shaking his head as Brooke answered, "Mike, I found the man I want and the drink I want too, a vodka tonic." Mike grinned and said, "Just checkin'" and walked toward the back bar.

Nathan felt an obligation to clear the air after the premature exit he made from Brooke's house the night before, but just as he started his apology Brooke put her hand on his leg and said, "I hope we're past last night's little disagreement."

He smiled and said, "Don't worry about it. One of these days I'll understand all of your Taoist stuff. I might not agree with it but I'm glad it makes you happy."

"Honey," she said, "it gives me peace and balance, that's all."

Nathan replied, "That's a lot." He knew his atheism made it harder to understand any kind of spiritual thinking, religious or otherwise. And he had been thinking a lot about Brooke's comments on his uncanny luck and how it seemed so out of balance. He wasn't sure what it all meant and, at least for the time being, he decided to avoid the topic in conversation.

"The Cardinals are down by three in the third quarter," he said, trying to change the subject.

Brooke looked at him, feigned excitement over his comment and said, "Uh . . . okay, thanks for the update."

Nathan knew she wasn't a big sports fan but she humored him when he wanted to watch a game or talk about the local teams. They ordered appetizers, talked about the activities of their upcoming week and quietly enjoyed the time together. He felt more relaxed than he had in weeks. He was glad that the subject of their moving in together didn't come up. It was off the table for a while, after a particularly blunt conversation led them both to realize the impact of such a decision. It wasn't just a discussion of their relationship which seemed solid in every respect, it was also a case of dealing with some very practical life issues like which one would have to sell a house, which one would have a much longer commute to work and which one would have no place to retreat if things didn't work out. They were both very independent people who had learned their own lessons from divorce. As much as they both wanted to take that big life-step toward each other, they also wanted to be very cautious.

After finishing lunch and enjoying one more drink, they paid Mike and walked out into the parking lot. "How did you manage to get the parking space closest to the door?" Brooke asked him.

"It opened up just as I was pulling in, where are you parked?"

Brooke pointed across the lot. "About six rows that way."

He walked her to her car and as they stood beside it he reminded her, "Don't forget about our non-refundable reservations for the hot air balloon ride next Saturday morning."

Brooke nodded and said, "Yeah, I remember. I was just hoping maybe you'd forget."

He smiled. "I know you're not crazy about heights, babe, but everyone talks about how safe those things are. It'll be the experience of a lifetime."

"If you say so," she said.

They kissed and held each other for what seemed like a whole minute to Nathan. He sensed that she didn't want to let go. "I'll call you tomorrow, babe," he said softly. She kissed him one more time and got into her Subaru. He stood and watched her back up and as she drove away he thought to himself that somehow that little car seemed to fit her organic, yoga, tofu-eating Taoist view of the world.

5

The workweek seemed to fly by. Nathan spent most of his time putting together contracts and marketing plans for Mesa Norte and had little time to read up on two more opportunities that Greg had brought to his attention. His string of successes seemed to be the focus of the office gossip. James had come up with a nickname for him: *Obiwan,* and the phrase *The Force is with Him.* His lucky streak was getting harder to ignore.

Nathan was looking forward to the weekend. He had planned every detail of the balloon adventure and the celebratory cookout afterward. It would be a perfect and unforgettable day. The only things left to do were to refill the propane tank on his gas grille and pick up the swordfish steaks at the market. Brooke was being a good sport by agreeing to be part of his hot-air balloon trip and he intended to make her a perfect dinner to commemorate the occasion.

He pulled into the Circle K parking lot and took his empty gas canister from his trunk. There was a clerk working by the open gate of the canister corral, and he took Nathan's empty can from him and said, "Pick whichever full one you want, sir." Nathan noticed a man waiting behind him for his own exchange, so he quickly chose a tank that looked clean and new, and walked into the store to pay for it. He stood in line behind the usual string of convenience store customers buying cheap 12-packs of beer, cigarettes and lottery tickets. Suddenly, an explosion rocked the front wall of the store and a spray of shattered glass rained down. There was a collective scream from the employees and customers and Nathan turned to see people rushing toward the propane tank enclosure outside. The entire parking lot was chaos.

The woman behind the cash register seemed torn between staying at her post and running outside to see what happened. A woman shouted, "Oh my God, a tank exploded, those poor men!" Somehow amidst the noise and confusion, the people in line managed to finish their transactions and hurry out of the store to become part of the crowd staring at the chaos on the sidewalk. Nathan paid for his fresh tank and carried it through the front door, trying to get his own view at what happened. He saw two employees in their red smocks, kneeling over the tank attendant and another man, both covered in blood. Nathan took a step to his right and saw that one of the men was the man who was waiting behind him for a new tank.

One of the inside employees, a young Latino man, had rushed outside to help and was pleading to the other, "I don't know what happened. It wasn't my fault! Somebody must have left a bleeder valve open on one of the tanks and static got to it or something like that. You gotta believe me man!."

Nathan saw the spreading pool of blood under the injured men, and noticed a shard of painted white metal from the canister imbedded in the stucco wall of the storefront. He figured it was that same type of jagged metal pieces that had ripped into the two unfortunate men.

A Phoenix police cruiser roared into the parking lot and he knew the paramedics wouldn't be far behind. He hurried to his car, laid his tank on the back seat, took a deep breath and as he headed home he tried to get the picture of those bloody, injured men out of his head. A random choice of a propane tank went in Nathan's favor and two other men were horribly injured. The only thing he could think was, "Why?" His constant good luck was becoming difficult to deal with and it was starting to rattle him.

Saturday morning was crystal clear and the temperature was seasonably cool at 5:00 AM. October was Nathan's favorite month; warm days, cool nights and unending blue skies. When he pulled into Brooke's driveway she was already standing at her front door waiting for him. "She seems eager, maybe she's over her fear of flying in a basket," he thought.

He got out of the car but she was already walking toward him. "Okay," she called out. "Let's do this." She seemed not so much excited as she was resolved to fulfilling a commitment.

On the way to the balloon field he told her about the propane tank accident and how he had luckily gotten his tank and was inside the store when the other man's tank blew up. He had no sooner finished telling her the events when he thought to himself, "Dumb move man, you shouldn't have brought it up, she's already scared enough and you're talking about an explosion and more of your good luck." He quickly changed the subject and talked about the things their friend Denis had told them. Denis was a former licensed balloon pilot and had flown this type of sunrise flight nearly a hundred times. He had told them how the early morning air was calm, how the winds were more predictable and how spectacular the desert looked as the sun came up over the mountains. Nathan was almost giddy with the anticipation of adventure while Brooke was trying to be a good sport and was clearly nervous. It was a half-hour drive to Deer Valley and the sun was barely showing itself over the edge of the mountains when their headlights showed the entrance gate to *Cloud Riders Ballooning*.

Nathan drove slowly along the dirt and gravel driveway, and as he reached the crest of a small hill he saw the glow of the propane flames illuminating two large balloons. "Wow, look at that!" he said looking over at Brooke.

She was looking at the closer of the two balloons, both of which were only partially inflated, and asked, "Which one is ours?"

"I don't know but I'll bet that guy will tell us."

He stopped the car as the tall, tanned, reed-thin man in a faded denim shirt walked over to his side of the car. "Mornin', are you Mr. Haas or Mr. McElroy?"

"I'm Mr. Haas, Nathan Haas. Where should I park?"

The man replied, "I'm Marty Robson, one of the pilots." He pointed to a chain link fence and said, "Right there is fine. Try to park close to the fence so we have enough room for the chase vehicles to line up."

Nathan made a wide U-turn and pulled alongside the fence, leaving just enough room for Brooke to open her door and get out. They gathered up their camera, jackets, sunglasses and a thermos of coffee and headed back toward the man. "Okay," Nathan called out, "which one is ours?"

Marty answered, "Well, they're both the same size and getting close to ready, so you get to pick."

Nathan looked over at Brooke, who still looked nervous. "What do you think, babe?"

Brooke looked over at a red and white striped balloon at the other end of the field, labeled *Adventurer,* then at the one in front of them, a yellow, green and red striped design with short, yellow tassels hanging from the skirt. It was called *Wind Song.* "Oh, honey, you decide," she said, clearly not as enthusiastic as Nathan was.

He looked at both balloons then turned to Marty. "We'll go with this one, I like the yellow tassels."

"Good choice," Marty said as he walked over to the basket. "This one's mine so I get to be your pilot, host and tour-guide this mornin'.

Another car pulled into the lot and a large Hispanic man pointed to the place where he wanted the driver to park. A middle-aged couple dressed in shorts and tee-shirts stepped out of the car. "Tourists I'll bet," Nathan said, obviously amused. "They think every square inch of Arizona is always hot. They're gonna freeze their asses off up there."

Nathan and Brooke walked over to a large wooden panel attached to the fence. Painted on it was a diagram of a hot-air balloon and all of its pieces and parts. The middle-aged couple walked over to join the group which now included the chase-team drivers and ground crew. Two burly Hispanic men held on to ropes, keeping the now-inflated balloons in place at their moorings. Everyone stood and listened as Marty went over a list of safety instructions and told them what to expect during the flight. Nathan had been talking to Brooke about the ride for nearly six months and she had looked at every ballooning website he could find for her. He hoped that knowing the details would ease her fears but so far it didn't look like anything had changed.

Their balloon towered over them as they walked toward it. Marty swung open the narrow gate of the wicker basket for them, and Brooke leaned over and whispered to Nathan, "I really must love you."

They stood at the edge of the basket and watched as Marty adjusted the control knobs on the three propane tanks. The basket was less than roomy. The three tanks and gear, along with three adults filled the floor space with little left over. Brooke looked up into the huge expanse of colorful vinyl fabric, glowing like a giant party decoration against the dark, early morning sky.

Nathan read the fear on her face. He put his arms around her and said, "Babe, this will be something you'll never forget." She gave him a weak smile, nodded and opened the lid of the thermos. Nathan saw the other couple enter their basket and wondered how soon they'd start to feel the cold morning air cut through their thin tee-shirts.

Marty leaned over the side of the basket, talking with the driver of the chase truck that would bring the balloon and basket back to the launch field at the end of the flight. The man holding the mooring rope smiled at Brooke and then winked at Nathan, as if he knew Brooke was more than a little nervous.

Marty turned back to them and called out, "Okay, ready when you are."

The noise from the propane jets made casual conversation difficult. Nathan put his arm around Brooke, smiled at Marty and said, "Let's go."

Marty waved to the man holding the mooring line. The man quickly coiled up the rope and tossed it into the basket, then ran around to the other side and did the same thing with the second line. Nathan was surprised at the suddenness of the balloon's upward climb. He looked down at Brooke's face as she clung to him. Marty saw her fearful expression and said, "Don't worry, miss, you'll be surprised how quickly you get used to it." Brooke, obviously unconvinced, managed a slight smile and nodded.

In minutes the balloon was floating above the rocky, scrub-filled hills north of central Phoenix. The sun was finally up over the mountains and the glow gave a yellowish orange hue to everything below them. Brooke seemed like she was starting to relax and stood looking out at the vast expanse of desert. Nathan noticed, at long last, signs of a smile on her pretty face. The wind tossed the tail of dark hair that stuck out the back of her baseball cap as she tried to focus her small camera. He stood beside her, his arm around her shoulders and enjoyed a view unlike any he had ever seen. Just as he felt they were settling in for the ride, he glanced over at Marty, who was holding his binoculars and looking back toward the launch field.

Nathan heard him say into the microphone of his headset, "I can't tell from here, what's your altitude?" Nathan took a small step toward Marty and leaned to his left, trying to see what Marty was looking at. He saw the red and white striped balloon about a mile behind them and at a much lower altitude. "Did you try turning off number three and re-igniting it?" he heard Marty ask. There was a brief pause and Marty said, "Number two's the same thing, oh shit man, that's not good."

Brooke had turned to see what the two men were looking at and she could tell from Marty's intense expression that something was wrong. She looked over at Nathan, who put his finger to his lips then pointed at the red and white balloon. Marty stopped his conversation long enough to check the gauges of his own balloon, then said "Make sure number one is on max. See if that's enough to climb. You're gonna need another couple hundred feet to get into the northeast flow. I'm in it right now." Marty realized that Nathan and Brooke were listening and said, "No need to worry, just a little problem with their rig, no big deal." His words seemed to put Brooke's mind at ease and she turned back to the other side of the basket to try another photograph. Nathan didn't buy Marty's comment. He had read up on ballooning and knew that when everything worked normally it was a safe activity but when something went wrong it could be very hard to fix it. Marty stood rigidly at the rim of the basket, his feet set at shoulder width and his elbows locked against his sides, trying to minimize his bodily motion. He was looking intently through his binoculars and trying to get a focus on the other balloon. "Okay Edgar, from what I can see your parachute valve is open a little too much," he said into his headset. "Can you see it from your angle?" He waited for Edgar's response, and then said, "Try to pull it closed, but don't jerk on the line, pull it slowly." There was another pause as Marty peered through his binoculars. "Shit," he muttered, "it didn't move."

Nathan didn't want to interrupt Marty but seeing the balloon in trouble and sensing that Brooke's fear was returning, he asked him, "Is this serious?"

Marty looked at him and nodded. "Sure looks like it. Two of his three tanks stopped working and the pressure valve at the top of the balloon won't move. He can't maintain altitude like that." Brooke gasped and put her hand over her mouth.

Marty checked his altimeter, then the gauges on his three tanks. "Everything is fine here," he said. "Don't you folks worry about a thing."

"What can we do to help them?" Brooke asked.

"Are you prayin' kind of folks?" Marty asked.

Nathan didn't respond and Brooke just gasped, "Oh no."

The red and white balloon was falling farther back by the minute and losing altitude at the same time. Nathan turned toward the west and scanned along the line they were headed. A long row of high-tension power lines glistened brightly in the morning sun. "Oh shit," he said.

"Oh shit is right," Marty replied. He held his binoculars in his left hand and pressed the microphone control on his headset. "Edgar, can you make it over those lines?"

Nathan was glad he couldn't hear the other end of the conversation. The scene on that balloon was probably total panic. He thought about the McElroys, the tourist couple who had probably been dreaming of their balloon adventure for a long time, and were now facing a potential catastrophe over the desert. He looked over at Brooke, who was now just as fixated on the red and white balloon as were Nathan and Marty. Nathan had worked so hard to convince her of the safety of their trip and the romance of floating over the foothills at dawn. Now they were both potential eyewitnesses to a looming tragedy.

Marty stood silently at the rail of the basket, his hands clenched on the binoculars, watching the other balloon drift helplessly toward the power lines. "Edgar, what's happening down there?" he asked, his voice grim and faltering. Whatever Edgar said in response was instantly painted on Marty's face. He pulled the binoculars away from his face, wiped his eyes with his right hand, and said softly, "God bless you all."

The next few minutes seemed to play out at half speed. Brooke clung tightly to Nathan, her face buried in his chest. Nathan was torn between watching the terrible events below him and turning away in a respectful gesture of acceptance of the fate of those three people. And in the middle of the painful moment was an awareness of the fact he chose to fly in *Wind Song*. Moored there in the dim, early morning light, the *Adventurer* looked just as exciting as *Wind Song*. It was basically a mental coin toss and he unknowingly chose the balloon that wasn't about to crash. Looking at three souls heading toward an unknown fate suddenly brought him to a strange realization; he was some kind of tipping point between the lucky and unlucky. He always seemed to be on the lucky side and people around him paid the price. Was that really how the world worked? Did luck always have a hand in the way life played out or was it just a series of strange coincidences? His recent lucky streak was definitely a fun ride and his choices and actions had made him a constant winner. He always came out on top and he always skirted trouble. It was the other guy who took the hit. Was this bizarre good fortune the way he was meant to go through life?

He snapped back to the moment when Marty cried out, "Oh God, please. Oh God, no" Nathan looked over the edge of the basket just in time to see the Adventurer, a small red and white image in the distance, come to a sickening halt as it struck the power lines. The balloon began to deflate almost instantly as the basket, its momentum still taking it forward, swung upward in a long arc. Nathan could barely make out the forms of the three people, brightly lighted by the sun against the backdrop of the sandstone hills, spilling out of the basket and falling toward the rocks and scrub on the desert below. Brooke had turned to look when she heard Marty's words, and the sight of the falling people made her turn back and bury her face in Nathan's jacket, her sharp cry of "No, no!" piercing the wind before she started sobbing.

Marty stood frozen, peering over the edge of the basket. His fingers fumbled with the control button on his headset, and he said in a surprisingly calm voice, "Miguel, this is *Wind Song*. We are beginning our descent immediately. Do you have rescue personnel en-route to Adventurer?"

The response to his message seemed to last for minutes and Nathan wondered what was being said as Marty's stood there, his ashen face totally without expression. Then Marty pulled the mouthpiece away from his face and snapped, "Okay folks, we're heading to a new landing sight. Please gather up your personal belongings and move to the other side of the basket."

He was direct, dispassionate, and, Nathan thought, totally in control of things. Nathan gently guided Brooke to the far edge of the basket as Marty pulled his headset back close to his mouth and began his instructions to the chase crew.

Under normal circumstances their descent would be an adventure unto itself, a deliberate but somewhat inexact prediction of where balloon and ground would meet. Ever since he'd first proposed a balloon ride to Brooke, Nathan had become fascinated with the blending of early scientific knowledge with modern aeronautics. Ballooning was a strange and wonderful coming together of the old and the new, of control and chance. But at this moment, what should have been a fascinating voyage of discovery and beauty had turned into tragedy. He and Brooke stood silently as Marty and the chase crew exchanged constant chatter on their headsets. They could see the dust from the three fast moving chase trucks far below them. Marty stood at the tanks, constantly adjusting the flow of gas and watching the tall, thin flame above him. His left hand held the cord to the parachute valve, and he expertly alternated the flow of fuel to the flame with the opening of the valve at the top of the balloon. He looked back and forth between the valve, the altimeter and the ground below. Their descent was steady, controlled and uneventful.

Nathan watched their shadow on the desert floor, looming closer and closer as Marty told them to hang on tightly to the rail. Brooke moved slightly to her left and braced her shoulder against Nathan. "Remember what Marty said in the training," he said to her calmly, "the basket sort of bumps along the ground until it comes to a stop, so just be ready for that."

She nodded, her face blank as she stared at the desert below. They seemed to be just a hundred feet or so off the ground and Nathan could see that their chase crew was already ahead of them, scrambling to get into position to grab the mooring lines. The wind was calm and their final minutes of flight were almost peaceful. They felt the basket skim over a clump of creosote bushes and then make its first easy contact with the ground. Marty's eyes were totally focused on the ground now, his left hand still working on the line to the parachute valve. The basket quickly slowed, bumped two more times on the dusty ground, then finally stopped when two men grabbed the mooring lines and pulled hard on them. One of the men wrapped his line around a steel bar attached to the bumper of a pick-up truck.

When the basket stopped moving, Marty swung open the gate and let Nathan and Brooke step out, then exited closely behind them. He quickly walked over to the driver of the lead truck. The men talked quietly with their heads down, and the rest of the crew went about their duties in total silence. The only sound, besides the screeching of a few circling hawks, was the chopping sound of a helicopter approaching from the south. Nathan could tell from its markings that it was a life-flight copter from one of the local hospitals. Just moments later two more choppers came into view and hovered in the distance over the area where the *Adventure*r had crashed. He turned to Brooke. "You okay, babe?"

She sighed, nodded and said, "Those poor people, do you think they're still alive?"

Nathan was reluctant to answer her, then after a long pause, said "I really doubt it, they fell a long way and it's all rock and sand."

It was a grim, silent ride back to the launch field. Nathan and Brooke rode in the back seat of the van, holding hands and listening to the chatter on the two-way radio. The last thing they heard as they climbed out in the parking lot was that the helicopter and fire department effort had turned from rescue to recovery. They gathered up their belongings, tossed everything on to the trunk of Nathan's car and drove back to Brooke's house. It hadn't been the day of adventure that Nathan planned, and the drive back was somber and almost totally without conversation.

6

When Nathan pulled into Brooke's driveway she turned toward him and asked, "Would you stay with me today?"

It was obvious she was still upset from the balloon crash, but he sensed there was something more. "Sure," he answered. "I was thinking the same thing myself."

They went into the house and Nathan walked through the kitchen and out to the patio while Brooke changed her clothes. It wasn't yet noon but he already felt like pouring himself a drink of something stronger than the lukewarm coffee from their thermos. A few minutes later Brooke joined him at the table, moving her chair just enough for her to find a patch of sunlight. "It's still kind of chilly," she said, leaning back and lifting her face toward the sun.

"Yeah," Nathan answered, "everything about this day gives me the chills."

"Are you hungry?" she asked. "I can make us a little something if you want."

"No thanks, I don't have much of an appetite, maybe later." They struggled to make small talk about the weather, Brooke's new garden and other trivial topics, as if they were trying to pretend the morning's events over the desert had never happened.

There was a brief lull in the conversation, then Brooke turned to face Nathan and said bluntly, "Honey, I really need to say something to you and I hope you don't get upset."

Nathan looked at her, his eyebrows raised, and asked, "What is it?"

She took a breath, hesitated a moment, a said, "honey, I know how you feel about some of my spiritual beliefs and the way I look at life. I know you don't buy into it but I want you to hear me out." He nodded as she continued. "We had a conversation a few days ago and I told you how I thought things were out of balance in your life. Your constant good fortune has made things so great for you and that makes me very happy. But I've been wondering about the people who weren't so lucky simply because you were."

Nathan sat in silence, letting her make her point. "There is a belief in some cultures that good fortune, let's call it luck, moves through the universe like a force. It requires an overall balance. There can't be night without day, there can't be warm without cold and there can't be good luck without bad."

He nodded and said, "Yeah, I know, we've talked about that many times."

"Yes, I know we have," she answered, "but what we haven't talked about is that these forces don't always flow evenly and all I have to do is watch you and listen to you to know that things are flowing around you and toward you in a very unnatural way."

Nathan was just as shaken by the events at the balloon park, and their silent drive back to Brooke's house had given him time to think about his latest bit of good luck. He had been hoping Brooke would want to talk because he was also starting to question his situation even though he didn't really understand it. When he heard her use the word *unnatural,* it struck a chord in him.

He remained silent, noticing the tense, determined look on Brooke's normally serene face. She continued. "This morning at the balloon park you were faced with a choice. You were asked to choose which balloon you wanted to ride in. Except for the color they were identical. And you made that decision without hesitating or questioning things. I believe that was the moment that forces were set in motion and those poor people's fate was set."

He interrupted, "Okay, I hear what you're saying, but why couldn't it have been a case where both balloons were okay, both flights were successful and nobody got hurt . . . or killed?"

Brooke answered him slowly. "Nathan, I think the positive forces around you are off-the-chart strong. It's like the normal amount of luck that follows people somehow got hyper-concentrated in you. Your luck, your good fortune is so strong and dominant that it requires an equally strong negative force to balance it out. You seem to be a focal point of good luck that brings bad luck to others in your sphere."

Nathan leaned back and slowly exhaled. "In my sphere, does that mean you think that just by my being in one balloon, the other one crashed, and that if I would have stayed home nothing bad would have happened to either of them?"

Brooke nodded, "Yep, that's what I think. I know it probably sounds crazy but with everything that's been happening around you I don't know what else to believe."

During the entire time they had known each other he and Brooke had shared little jokes, disagreements and debates on the idea of yin yang. Nathan wanted nothing to do with any kind of religion, and when Brooke reminded him that Taoism wasn't a religion but more of a philosophy or belief system, he felt she was just splitting hairs. But now he had to admit that something strange was at work. Good luck, bad luck, Yin and yang, Karma or Juju, it was all just plain weird and way beyond unsettling. He seemed to be living a charmed life, a charmed life that brought pain to people around him. There were just too damned many coincidences to ignore what seemed to be all too obvious to Brooke.

Nathan looked into Brooke's eyes, swallowed, and said, "I'm really wondering about all of this too. Don't think for a minute that everything that's happened lately hasn't scared the livin' shit out of me. It's almost like I'm hurting people just by being me."

Brooke's expression had turned to one Nathan had never seen before: almost panic. "Honey, I don't want you to take this the wrong way or think I don't love you, because you know I do." He froze, waiting for her to continue. "You have to stop and think this whole thing through. Everything you do, every decision you make, and everywhere you go is causing an imbalance. Your good luck is bad luck for everyone else, and I'm scared."

Nathan desperately wanted to come up with one of his tried and true responses to Brooke's spiritual comment, a glib phrase to counter her point. Something like, "Come on, it's no big deal, it's just a coincidence," or "Give it time and things will all balance out." But with everything that had happened in the past few weeks, he knew she wouldn't accept his answer because he couldn't accept it himself. Brooke's grim expression and her tone of voice made it obvious that she was struggling to understand what was going on and he sat quietly and let her continue.

"Honey, I want you to understand that anything I say is because I care deeply for you and I want a future with you."

"And I feel the same way," he replied. She sat silently, looking down and wringing her hands and the longer she didn't speak the more nervous he got.

Finally she stood up, walked over to his chair and knelt on the patio in front of him. She took his hands in hers, kissed them, looked him right in the eye and said, "Nathan, I love you but I'm afraid to be near you."

Her words hit him like a punch in the stomach. He just looked at her, trying to get a read on her meaning, as she continued. "We've talked about this so many times in so many ways and it still comes down to the fact you're living some kind of charmed, unnatural life, a life that keeps you safe and hurts others, a life that sees you win while everyone else loses."

Nathan nodded, knowing she was right and he also knew there was no point pretending it was anything else. After a long and very uncomfortable pause, he said, "I can understand why you're scared because I am too, but you have to remember that the people around me who've been hurt . . . or killed, were mostly strangers. Lots of the people I'm with on a regular basis haven't had anything bad happen to them."

"I understand that," Brooke answered, "but that doesn't mean it couldn't happen, or won't."

Those last few words sent a chill down Nathan's back. He wondered what would happen to him next, where he would be safe and someone would be hurt. What if something horrible happened to Brooke simply because she was with him? How about James or someone else in his office? What if something worse than a stuck elevator happened and seriously hurt people he cared about?

He leaned forward and kissed Brooke's forehead. "Babe, I don't want to lose you because of this," he said calmly.

She gripped his hands tightly and said, I don't want to lose you either, but there are forces at work here that take our feelings out of play. We have to be realistic about what this all means."

He shook his head and stood up. "It means I'm a fucking pariah," he said bitterly. "I can't live a normal life knowing that people will suffer just from my being around them."

Brooke stood up and put her arms around his waist. He could feel her trembling as they clung to each other, and he was trembling just as hard. He knew his idyllic little life was too perfect to be anything close to normal from now on. He looked down at Brooke and said, "Babe, I know you're not the

Dalai Lama or a mystic or anything like that, but you're the only one who has a clue about what's going on here. Will things eventually change? Will my luck ever turn bad or at least start to balance out?"

Brooke leaned back in his arms and looked at him intently. "There is no way to know. The fact that the life forces around you are so skewed right now makes me think it will take a long time to find a balance, if they ever do."

He saw the tears welling up in Brooke's eyes and it triggered tears of his own. They clung tightly to each other without speaking. Finally he relaxed his arms and Brooke took a small step back. "Okay," he said calmly. "Let's figure this out. We're two smart people, and there must be some kind of answer to this problem."

She looked at him, her eyes red from crying. "Let's try it long distance for a while. Phone calls, e-mails and text messages. Let's see what goes on around you without my being a physical part of things."

Nathan hung his head and then looked into her eyes. "You know, this really sucks."

She nodded. "I know it does but we . . . I really mean you, have to be careful and watchful from now on. No high-risk adventures . . ."

"What, like going to Walgreens or buying propane?" he asked sarcastically.

Brooke knew he was frustrated and hurting and didn't take offense. "Honey, just be extra careful and extra focused on everything and everyone around you for a while and maybe things will change direction."

"You mean maybe my luck will change?"

Brooke smiled, hugged him again and said, "Let's go inside and I'll make us some lunch."

He couldn't help but wonder if it would be their last meal together as a couple.

7

Nathan's new lifestyle was a work in progress and there wasn't much that remained of his old routine. He and Brooke were making the best of avoiding physical contact, but phone calls and text messages were poor substitutes for talking face-to-face and being together. He had figured out a driving route to the office that avoided major highways and fast moving traffic. Even the simple tasks of his life like working in his yard and buying groceries had become slow, almost choreographed rituals. His work environment was pretty much the same as it was but he found he'd become tentative in making decisions and, at times, almost timid. All in all he didn't feel like himself anymore. He was doing his best to stay under the radar of the normal deal making team and even though he was still closing deals, he was only working on the safe and easy ones. No high profile projects, no spotlight and no controversy.

His leisure time was the hardest part to handle. Without Brooke, he was spending more time alone or with friends he hadn't been with much for a long time. He sought out James a few times to join him for a beer but when James suggested a mountain bike ride or a hike in the high desert, Nathan made up excuses to avoid it. All he could picture was the two of them riding on a narrow path in the hills and James' bike slipping off the edge and falling downhill on to the rocks. How long could he pretend everything was normal? How long before his friends stopped calling him? And most importantly, how long could he maintain a romantic relationship with Brooke without being with her? He was starting to feel the effects of his self-imposed exile, and he knew that, sooner or later, he'd have to test his situation. It had been well over three weeks since the balloon accident and nothing bad had happened to anyone around him. Was it because of his limited exposure to people and activity, or could it be because his luck was changing? He remembered that Brooke said it could take a long time to change, but how long was long?

With the work week over Nathan wondered what the weekend would be like, but the reality of his commute was a more immediate concern. "Geez, it's Friday," he thought as he tried to navigate his new route home from the office, "the traffic is never this heavy on Fridays". He tried to get a look up ahead of the car in front of him to see if he could find out why things weren't moving but couldn't see anything but a dozen or so other cars in the same predicament. Since it looked like he'd be stuck in place for a while he grabbed his cellphone from the console and called Brooke. Her number had no sooner come up on the screen when he heard a siren up ahead and then, surprisingly, the traffic started creeping forward again. He turned off his radio when he heard Brooke's answer the phone. "Hi babe," he said, knowing he couldn't hide the loneliness in his voice.

"Hi," she replied softly, "are you on your way home?"

He hesitated as he picked up speed with the now near-normal pace of the traffic. "Yeah," he said, "the traffic is starting to let up a little and I was thinking how I usually head right to your house for Friday Happy Hour."

Brooke chuckled and said, "You mean Friday Happy all night long." Her voice was comforting to him and he realized how more than ever he really needed to see her.

"You know," he said, "It's been nearly a month, and no accidents, no disasters, no trouble at work and nobody got hurt. I miss you so much and I'm tired of living like some kind of leper."

Brooke sighed and asked, "So what's your point?"

He answered, "My point is I think we should get together . . . tonight, and talk about where all of this is going."

Brooke sighed again and said, "Oh honey, I don't know. It's so hard to be sure about something like this."

"I know, I agree," he answered, "but it seems to me that things are different now."

There was a long break in the conversation and then Brooke finally said, "Well, I guess you're right. There's no way of being sure one way or the other but let's keep it simple, why don't you just come over here and we'll order pizza?"

He let out a sigh of relief. "Good plan, I'll stop and get some wine, how about a nice Pinot Noir?"

"Yeah, that sounds . . . good," she replied. He could hear the nervousness in her voice

Nathan's remembered that his new route home took him past Cave a Vins, an upscale wine store that he had been eager to visit. His dinner with Brooke, simple as it sounded on the phone, was still very important to him, almost like a test of their relationship. And he knew that, beyond their relationship, it was also a test of how safe it was for her to be around him. He was frustrated and worried. Going nearly a month without a catastrophe was the way life was supposed to be. That was normal and here he was, ready to buy an expensive bottle of wine to celebrate a month of being normal.

After a few minutes he saw the sign for the wine shop and moved into the right lane. There were only three cars in the parking lot and he figured he could be in and out quickly. He parked beside a rusty blue Dodge with two men sitting in it, grabbed his cellphone from the console and went into the store. It was a cozy little place, with dark oak shelves packed full of what seemed to be an endless variety of wine. He stood just inside the front door, looking around to get his bearings when a smiling young woman in a crisp white blouse and black slacks approached him. "How can I help you sir?" she asked.

"Well, you can point me toward a nice Pinot Noir," he answered.

The woman led him down a short aisle and said, "Here you go, we have some great deals on a couple of new French varietals, and this section is all California."

"Thanks," he said, "I'll just check out what you have."

The woman smiled and walked back to the front of the store. He enjoyed looking through the selection and seeing wines he had never even heard of, but the prices were higher than he was used to paying. "Oh what the hell," he thought, "this is a special occasion."

He read a small sign describing what sounded like a very nice 2008 Sonoma Coast offering, took one bottle from the shelf then headed toward the checkout. As he turned the corner into the main aisle, a short, gray haired man nearly ran into him. They both stopped, as if deciding who had the right of way, and Nathan said, "Go ahead, I'm not in a hurry." The man smiled and stepped forward, and as Nathan followed behind him, he heard the young woman in the crisp, white blouse scream. He looked up and saw her behind the cash counter, her face ashen as a man in a black stocking cap pointed a small handgun toward her. The gray haired man was looking down at the two bottles of wine he was carrying and by the time he reacted and looked up to see what was going on he was just a few feet from the man with the gun.

The next few moments were like a blur. Nathan lunged to his right behind a small display of stemware. The man with the gun turned and shot the gray haired man in the chest and he crumpled to the floor, his bottles crashing on the tile and sending a flood of red wine across the aisle. Nathan dashed toward a door that he'd guessed led to the back storage room. He heard the gunman snarl, "Hurry up, give me the fuckin' money," and the young woman started to cry. Nathan ducked into the small room, turned and placed his foot against the bottom of the door and stood still, trying to hear what was going on at the front of the store. He heard the chime on the entrance door ring so he knew someone had either entered the store or the gunman had left. The only thing he heard was the woman crying, and nothing else. He pushed the door open just enough to peer out and he could see the woman shaking and slouching over the counter, sobbing uncontrollably. He heard what sounded like squealing tires and a car horn, and he assumed it was the gunman and his friend, probably the other guy in the blue Dodge.

He walked slowly and cautiously toward the front of the store, looking in every direction for signs of trouble. A glance out the window showed that the blue Dodge was gone. When he got to the main aisle he looked down and saw the gray haired man face down on the floor, a pool of blood spreading around him, mixing with the puddle of wine. Nathan ran to the woman. "Are you alright?" he asked, trying to regain his composure. The woman was still sobbing and just nodded to him. Nathan took his cellphone from the holster on his belt and called 911. He bent down over the man on the floor trying to be calm and explain the situation to the 911 operator. His heart was racing and through the terror of what had happened came a sickening feeling; his luck hadn't changed at all.

An EMS wagon and a police cruiser arrived almost simultaneously, and Nathan stood beside the young woman as the EMTs worked on the wounded man. He watched their skillful movements as he did his best to describe to the police what had happened. The wounded customer was wheeled out on a gurney just as a tall, Arab looking man rushed in. The man told the police that he was the owner and one of the cops steered him to a corner and questioned him. Within a half hour the police wrapped up their on-site activities and Nathan was struck by how routine it seemed to them. A man had been shot and a store robbed, and the police on the scene seemed to take it all in stride, like it was just another day at work for them. The officer in charge walked over to Nathan and handed him a business card. "Mr. Haas, here's how you can get in touch with me if you think of anything else you haven't already told us."

Nathan took the card and nodded. "Thank you, I will," he said.

The officer nodded, paused, and then said, "Mr. Haas, what happened here was a terrible thing, I'm sure you realize how lucky you are that you didn't get shot too."

Nathan looked at him, then looked out the window at the flashing lights of the EMS van, and answered, "Yeah, I'm one lucky guy."

He made the drive back to his house almost without thinking or being aware of anything around him. It was like he was totally numb. He pulled into the garage, turned off the engine and sat for a moment. Finally, he gathered up his laptop case, sport coat and the bottle of wine and went into his house. Still not able to focus or clear his mind, he set the wine on the kitchen counter and walked into his bedroom, He stood there for a moment, glancing mindlessly around the room, and then laid his laptop case on his dresser, kicked off his shoes and laid down on the bed. He lost track of the time as he stared at the ceiling. Except for the pounding of his heart he felt nothing else. His hands shook as he took off his tie and dropped it on to the floor. He lay there, feeling trapped, thinking about Brooke, about his job and about everything that had happened in the past few months. Then he took a deep breath, slowly exhaled and muttered, "Yep, I'm one lucky son of a bitch."

"The Almost Life of Leonard Paduszka"

Saturday May 19th

Daniel and Jess waited until they saw John Sherman's car pull out of the parking lot and on to the highway before they walked back to the clubhouse and into the grill room. When John suggested they all share a drink after their round of golf Daniel quickly begged off, saying that he had to get home to finish some paperwork. Daniel had been working as a consultant to John at Franchise Holdings for almost two years. The excuse about doing paperwork was a total lie, but, as much as Daniel valued his out-of-the-office opportunities with his client, he couldn't bear spending another minute with Archie Baggins. Baggins was a short, overweight blowhard with more money than social skills, and John had asked Daniel to join them for a round of golf to help cement a deal that had been in the works for months. John had developed a plan for Baggins to purchase a major interest in two regional fast-food franchises that wanted to go national. He brought Daniel into the mix to work with both groups and John was counting on him to help sink the hook into Baggins' checkbook.

"Hey, man, thanks again for filling out the foursome," Daniel said to Jess as they walked toward the bar.

"No problem," Jess replied, "at least it's no problem as long as you're sure you can comp my greens fees."

"Relax," Daniel snapped, "I told you I can cover it, just give me a week or so to get you paid back."

The two men sat at the end of the bar and Daniel signaled to the barmaid while Jess turned in his stool to scope out the room. "Any prospects?" Daniel asked, noticing the intent look on Jess' face.

"Not right now, but it's still early." Jess answered. "The married women go out in the morning with their friends and husbands. The hot babes tee off later so they can finish when its an appropriate time to drink alcohol."

Daniel replied, "Its seven minutes after noon on a Saturday, and as far as I'm concerned it's freaking Happy Hour."

Daniel and Jess were former roommates and had been friends for a long time. Daniel knew every detail of Jess' strategy to search for, find, romance and marry a rich widow or divorcee. Jess worked for a graphics and printing company but was going nowhere in terms of his future. Marrying a woman of means was his career goal in lieu of a real job or a retirement plan. When Jess first explained it to Daniel it seemed funny, but it wasn't long before he realized that Jess was totally serious. He was on a mission to find the female equivalent of a sugar daddy, his own "sugar mommy". As Daniel was turning back toward the bar a tall blonde woman caught his eye. "Hey," he said to Jess, "far right corner, by the window, four at the table, tall blonde on the left, white blouse, any thoughts?"

Jess scanned that part of the room, locked his gaze and squinted. "Hmm, not bad, not bad at all, nice looking, classy, decent chest, can't tell much about the rest of her body until she stands up, but definitely worth keeping an eye on."

The barmaid walked up and said, "Hello Mr. Warren," and Daniel answered, "Hi Justine, they got you back working on weekends I see."

"Yeah, she replied, I miss being home with the kids but I'm making more money, so what can I say?"

They ordered their drinks and Daniel did his best to get Jess' impressions of the golf outing and their partners while Jess kept half of his brain on the blonde. "So what did you think of Archie Baggins?" Daniel asked.

"A total asshole," Jess answered, "he thinks he's got some kind of fuckin' people radar or something."

"Yeah," Daniel agreed, "he seems to think he invented demographics and market analysis."

Justine set their beers in front of them and, as Daniel took a sip Jess had turned his head and said matter-of-factly, "Oh good, she's standing up, looks like she has a nice butt, nice legs too. She definitely has promise."

Daniel shook his head at his friend's crudeness, looked at the woman, paused and said, "Oh geez, sorry man. I see a very large diamond on her left hand, looks like some other handsome young man has captured her heart."

Jess swiveled back to face the bar. "Shit," he muttered, genuinely displeased.

Daniel switched back to his earlier line of thought. "So I've got to put together a report to get this Baggins guy to agree to an investment contract. I have to come up with something big, something that he'll look at and say, "show me where to sign."

Jess took a long, slow drink of his beer, set the glass back down on the bar, looked at Daniel and said, "Come on, man, you just spent a few hours with a total egomaniac asshole who thinks he has his fat, stubby fingers on the pulse of the American consumer. He said flat out that all he needs to predict a person's spending habits are the guy's ethnic background and a few bits of data. So kiss his fat little ass, tell him he's a genius and slide a contract in front of him."

Daniel shook his head. "Nope, this guy needs to see the numbers and I'm not sure I can get him enough history on the franchises to sway his thinking. Man, I gotta get out of this line of work."

Jess had swiveled back toward the corner of the room. The blonde was leaving with her friends and Jess lifted his glass in her direction. "Farewell my lovely, if you only knew what we could have had together."

Daniel smiled, unsure of how serious or how lighthearted Jess' toast was meant to be. "Hey," he said, "I really need your help here man."

"I know you do," Jess answered, turning back to face the bar. "Just give me a second to reflect on another love lost, will you'?"

Daniel couldn't help but grin. He looked at Jess, wondering if and when his potty-mouthed friend would ever get serious about his life.

"So," Jess started, "you said you don't have much history to convince this jerk that he should invest."

"Yeah," Daniel answered, "that's about it."

Jess sipped his beer and said, "Then just make up some shit."

Daniel looked at him, not sure how to respond,. "And by that I assume you mean make up some phony numbers, some phony statistics." Jess nodded. "I can't do that, you idiot, its illegal,"

Jess nodded again and replied, "Yeah, it's illegal, but it seems like the kind of thing nobody could ever verify. How many greasy chilidogs did ABC Place sell in the third quarter last year? How many tanker-loads of cola did XYZ Place pour down people's throats last year? You're talkin' about shit that sounds so damn believable. I mean, who would ever question the kind of consumption that this trailer park country of ours displays on a daily basis?"

Daniel was irritated by Jess' seemingly flippant answer to his problem, but he was also embarrassingly intrigued by the basic premise. He had to admit that the kind of franchises he was helping to promote were firmly rooted in a cheap, unhealthy lifestyle. Was it really so hard to believe that anyone would question the number of things people would spend their money on when they were inexpensive and easy to get? When Jess got up to go to the restroom, Daniel sat there thinking. Made up statistics. Made up demographics. Made up consumer feedback. It all seemed so obvious, and it all seemed so easy to pull off.

When Jess got back to the bar Daniel said, "You know, as much as I hate to admit it, I think you're on to something here with this fake statistics idea."

Jess climbed up on to his stool and said, "And you know, I was standing there in the urinal, making room for the next round, when I got this other really cool idea."

Daniel looked over at him, waiting for what would most likely be another torrent of bizarre wisdom, but Jess just sat there, sipping the last inch of his beer. Daniel waited a moment, and then said, "Okay, so tell me this big idea." Before Jess could answer, Daniel signaled to Justine for another round, and then repeated, "Okay, let's hear it."

"Well," Jess started, "it seems like you live in a world of charts and graphs and consumer bullshit, am I right?"

Daniel nodded, "Yeah, and thanks for making my job seem so romantic."

"Okay," Jess continued, "so you can fudge the numbers to make them say what you want. You can tweak the details to say what the people want to hear. But, if you really, truly want to make an impact, you need to create that perfect example of someone who knows your customer. Call him Joe Chilidog or Joe Tater Tot or whatever, but come up with a franchising genius, the guy who speaks for everyone in the trailer park."

Daniel paused and then said, "You mean create an expert, a fake one."

"Yeah," Jess answered, almost annoyed that Daniel hadn't picked up on the obviousness of his idea, "You deal with statistics, social media, all kinds of marketing shit, how hard would it be to create a person, an expert on the an average American consumer, a guy that you can totally control?"

Daniel leaned back in his barstool, looked at Jess, and said, "I have to pee, I'll be back in a minute." As he walked to the restroom he thought about Jess' idea of creating a person. Not a real person, just a persona, an identity of someone who could represent whatever Daniel wanted him to. He thought about the questionable information that was touted as fact in the media. Innuendo was considered truth. Rumors were spread around the globe before anyone gave any thought to actually checking for their veracity. The public was gullible and willing to accept almost anything simply because they saw it on TV or read it on the internet. And he figured Archie Baggins was no different.

He stood at the urinal, experiencing the same kind of clarity and inspiration that Jess had found looking down into the porcelain. He would figure out an honest way to lock up Archie Baggins and his very large bank account, but there was much more potential in creating this new persona, this new person, as real and genuine as Daniel chose to make him. He walked back toward the bar and saw Jess eyeing a very attractive older woman who was standing in the doorway. Daniel had joined the club just a few months earlier and didn't know many of the members yet, and he had never seen the woman before. As he passed her they exchanged smiles and hellos. When he reached the bar Jess asked him, "How does she look up close?"

"Very nice," Daniel said, "I'm guessing between 45 and 50." Then he stopped, realizing that he sounded like some kind of matchmaker or love pimp for Jess.

Justine set the second round on the bar along with two menus. Having lunch today Mr. Warren?" she asked.

"Hmm, I don't know," Daniel replied and turned to Jess. "You have time for lunch?"

Jess answered without taking his eyes off the woman, "Sure." Daniel said,

"Justine, this love struck young man is my friend Jess Katzenbaugh."

Jess turned to face her, wondering if she realized he had been ogling one of the female members. "Nice to meet you Justine," he said, smiling sheepishly.

They looked over the menus and ordered, and Daniel said, "I gotta tell you, your idea of creating a person is strange and twisted but I like it . . . a lot."

"Yeah, I thought you would," Jess answered.

Daniel said, "I think instead of fudging the sales data, which could get John in trouble and make me lose my contract, I'll work on creating this guy, this Joe-Expert who can offer his opinion and experience on any subject I choose. He'll look, sound and act real, and I can use him with other clients too." Jess smiled, obviously pleased that Daniel was actually impressed with his idea.

The two of them sat at the bar, eating their lunches and talking about their soon to be born creation. They agreed the person should be male because his personality and opinions would be built on their own traits and experience. The name took a lot longer. Jess wanted to go for a youthful, trendy sounding name like Lance or Matthew, but Daniel held out for a name with more gravitas. After all, as he explained to Jess, this person would have to look intelligent, successful and accomplished, otherwise his comments and opinions wouldn't be as credible. He had to speak for people outside of the trailer park as well. And it wouldn't hurt if his last name had an ethnic flavor that added to his common man image. They agreed he should be in his late 40s, old enough to have accomplished things in life but still young enough to be open to new ideas.

They went through a list of first names, trying to find one that was not too common but not strange sounding either. Michael, Robert and James were too common. Howard and Oscar sounded too old. Then Daniel thought that names from his father's generation would fit the timeline and blurted out "Leonard!"

Jess pondered the name for a moment then said, "Sounds about right, now how about his last name."

"Well," Daniel replied, "we agreed he shouldn't be a WASP."

"Yeah," Jess agreed, "we need something that sounds like he came from hard working immigrant stock."

They shared dozens of surnames of people they'd known in their pasts but nothing clicked. "Then, after a brief pause, Daniel said, "I had a high school teacher, Mr. Paduszka, he was Polish, a really nice guy."

"Leonard Paduszka, Leon-ard Pa-dusz-ka," Jess said in clipped syllables. "Sounds like a really solid citizen to me."

"Leonard Paduszka," Daniel said. He lifted his beer glass toward Jess and Jess met it with his own. "To Leonard Paduszka!"

Sunday May 20th

The sound of rainfall and thunder woke Daniel much earlier than his usual Sunday morning routine called for. He rolled to his right and saw that the noise hadn't bothered Maggie, her light snoring unbroken by the noise outside. It had only been three months since she moved into his house and getting used to her snoring was one of the small adjustments he was trying to make. He sat up and looked down at her pretty face and the wild red curls of her hair spread across her pillow. He always had a fondness for redheads and when he met Maggie he fell for her fast and hard. Her creamy skin and auburn hair were a big contrast with his dark hair and tan. He bent down and kissed her cheek three times, a little gesture that had become part of their morning routine, then got out of bed and walked into the kitchen.

After getting a pot started in the coffee maker he went out into the rain and rain, picked up the plastic-wrapped Sunday newspaper then hurried back inside, his wet t-shirt clinging to his body. When the coffee was ready he poured himself a cup and sat down at the counter. He usually dove right in to reading the paper but this morning a bright yellow file folder on the counter was distracting him. His barroom conversation and brainstorming session with Jess had so inspired him that he had spent Saturday afternoon and part of the evening

putting together a plan to create Leonard Paduszka. The idea
had energized him in a way he hadn't felt in a very long time.
His job of building business plans for franchise investors didn't
exactly stimulate the left side of his brain, and Jess' idea of
creating an identity for a person who didn't exist was the kind
of creative challenge he needed. He was a writer and a thinker
at heart, and his strong opinions on most everything in life were
hard to contain when he was at the office. He gathered up the
newspaper, slid it off to the side of the counter and opened the
yellow folder.

"Don't tell me you're working on a Sunday morning,"
Maggie said, brushing back a wisp of red from her forehead as
she walked into the room.

"Mornin' honey," Daniel said. "Nope, it's not work, just
that little idea Jess and I came up with."

"Oh yeah," she replied as she poured her coffee, "the faux
man." She sat down on the stool across from Daniel and sorted
through the sections of newspaper then glanced over at Daniel
as he intently read one of the pages he'd pulled from the folder.
"Wow, you're really into that." she said

He put the page back into the folder and closed it, then,
embarrassed, said, "Yeah, I'm sure you think it's a weird idea but
I can't stop thinking about it."

"Well," she answered, "let's just say it's unusual, but I have
to admit it's kind of interesting too."

Daniel sipped his coffee then opened the folder again.
"Honey," he started, paused and said, "just think for a minute
about the way we meet people and the way we view what goes
on around us."

Maggie took a long, slow sip of coffee and said, "I'm not
sure I get your point."

"Okay," he replied, "here's an example. You're on Facebook
and Twitter. You have a personal e-mail and another account at
your office. You tell me about all of the blogs you read." Maggie
nodded. "So," Daniel continued, "add up all that activity in a

week or a month. How many of those people you encounter in all those ways do you know personally?"

"Geez," she answered, thinking it over a moment, "I guess about ten or twenty percent."

"Okay," Daniel said, "now think about the other eighty or ninety percent. How many of them do you know for sure are legitimate. Real people. Verifiable people. How many?"

Maggie hesitated, trying to come up with a plausible answer. "I don't know," she said slowly, "all of them, most of them, I don't know."

"There you go," Daniel said sharply. "You take on faith that all of those people exist but you really don't know for sure."

"So where are you going with this?" she asked.

"I'm not exactly sure, it's still a work in progress."

"Well, like I said it's an interesting idea, but it sounds like you could really get into trouble doing it."

"Honey," we don't intend to extort money or commit fraud or do anything illegal with Leonard."

"Geez," she answered, "you already sound like you think he's real."

Daniel leaned back, put his hands on top of his head, grinned and said, "Leonard is real, as real as anyone else that you've never met in person."

"Please honey," she said, looking Daniel right in the eye, "please be careful, be very, very careful."

Daniel opened the folder again and pulled out the top page of the papers in it. "Here, look at this list." Maggie read down the page and read aloud what he had written. "**Name**, Leonard Allen Paduszka. **Born**, Rockford, Illinois, September 14, 1965. **Graduated**, Magna Cum Laude, University of Chicago, BA in Business, MBA, Thunderbird Academy of International Business. **Occupation**, Financial Planner and Consultant. **Marital Status,** Divorced, no children. **Residence**, 1433 North Oakbrook Circle, Chicago, Illinois 66122." She looked up at Daniel and asked, "Is that a real address?"

"Nope," he answered, "it's a fake street number next door to an old warehouse downtown."

"Okay, so he has a name and an address, what else?"

Daniel smiled. "Jess and I are going to meet after work tomorrow and decide how we'll split the rest of the steps."

"What steps?"

"Well we got the easy part done, the basic framework, the back story if you will. Now we have to flesh things out. Leonard has to express himself now."

"Express himself?"

"Yeah, here's this educated, upper-middle class guy who needs to tell us his story."

"And you and Jess are going to write the story?" Daniel grinned and nodded.

Maggie got up and walked to the coffee maker. "Need a warm-up?" she asked.

"Sure," he said, holding his cup as she refilled it.

She filled her own cup and sat back down. "So how do you and Jess decide what his story is going to be?"

"Well," he replied, "Jess thinks we have to go into a lot of detail, make every little decision about what Leonard thinks and feels, how he lives his life, all of that stuff."

"And I take it you disagree," she said.

"Yeah, I think all we need are a few more basic things and then we push Leonard out of the nest."

Maggie looked at him, puzzled by his comment. "Push him where?"

Daniel shuffled through the papers in the yellow folder again, found the one he wanted and handed it to her. "This is how Leonard gets introduced to the world. After that, the world decides for itself who and what he is."

Maggie looked over the outline he had created, a hand-written list of items and comments that would set the stage for the birth of Leonard Paduszka. "Wow," she said, "this is pretty ambitious." Before Daniel could say anything else, she added, "And some of it looks illegal." She looked at him with a skeptical face. "Honey, like I said before, this could get you in trouble, I mean like legal trouble."

"And like I said before, I don't think so," he replied. "We have no intention of using any of this to steal from somebody or harm anyone in any way."

Maggie looked at the outline again. She was working as a research assistant in a law firm until she finished her studies in Business. She was not shy about expressing her negative feelings about lawyers and, through her brief experience in the field, she understood the serious nature of what Daniel could get himself into. Given the fact she worked with lawyers he had already expected her to find a dark cloud behind the silver lining. Maggie looked up from her reading. "Okay here's an example of what I mean. "You say here you're going to create Leonard's birth certificate and a Social Security card. That's clearly illegal and there are some very ugly penalties attached."

"Yeah," Daniel answered, "I guess in and of itself it's illegal but if we don't use that information for anything other than to establish an identity, who would know and who would ever say it's wrong? It's like the old saying, *No harm no foul.*"

Maggie shook her head. "Honey, you're splitting those hairs pretty fine."

"Maybe so," he said, "but trust me, we don't intend to use Leonard in any way that's illegal or fraudulent. They'll just be pieces of paper in a file folder."

Maggie sighed and said, "Okay, I trust you." She paused, then asked, "I'm probably going to regret this, but is there any way I can help you?"

Monday May 21st

Jess was already sitting at a table in the back corner of *Rockford's* when Daniel arrived. "Sorry, man," he said to Jess as he dropped into the chair across from him, "long day in franchise land."

"No problem," Jess replied, "I just got here myself." A heavy-set young woman suddenly arrived tableside and asked, "Can I get you gentlemen something to drink?" Daniel ordered a vodka tonic and Jess asked for a Black and Tan, and when the woman walked away Daniel said excitedly, "Man, I have got some great ideas for Leonard."

"Me too," Jess answered, "this thing is going to be so cool."

For the next half hour they shared their ideas and expanded the strategy outline that Daniel had started. Jess talked about how a guy who worked with him at the graphics shop had agreed to help him with the fake documents as long as Jess paid him fifty dollars and promised not to tell anyone about his involvement. Daniel balked at paying anyone to get involved but as they talked things through, he realized there would have to be some kind of financial investment. Since Daniel would be the one who would actually be using Leonard's identity, he agreed to give Jess the money. They decided that any expenses beyond that had to be discussed and agreed to in advance.

Daniel was most excited by an ironic twist of fate that had occurred in his family. His father's brother, Daniel's Uncle Dave, had died in January of a heart attack. Daniel's father was executor of the estate and had possession of the things that Dave hadn't bequeathed to anyone or weren't worth enough to sell. Among the leftovers was a box of miscellaneous photographs, letters and personal memorabilia that Dave had accumulated in his 47 years of life. When a proper period of mourning had passed Daniel sat with his father and went through the entire box. Among the remnants and remembrances of his uncle's life were his birth certificate and Social Security card. Daniel had been fairly close to his uncle and had expressed his desire to have a few of the photos and things. His father told him to take whatever he wanted but so far he hadn't gotten around to it.

Jess listened as Daniel told him about the box, and when Daniel finished, Jess said, "Amazing, that is so amazing, man.

Everything we need to do can be built from a birth certificate and Social Security card."

"What do you mean everything we need to do? Keep in mind, none of this can be tied to anything illegal."

"I know, man, you don't have to keep reminding me. I just mean that Leonard needs to be born and officially registered as a citizen of the United States, and you can make that happen, sort of. Get me those things and my friend at work can scan them and work on them and make Leonard real."

The two men drank, talked quietly enough so no one could hear their conversation, and broke down the responsibility for the things that needed to be done. Daniel would give the birth certificate and Social Security card to Jess, and Jess would pay his friend to scan them and reproduce them with Leonard's name. Daniel would create an e-mail account in Leonard's name and begin sending messages and comments to the newspapers, magazines and websites. Maggie had agreed to set up Facebook, Twitter and Instagram accounts and to send out messages to as many people as possible. "Wait a minute," Jess said. "How does Leonard get friends on Facebook when he doesn't exist, he doesn't know anyone?"

"Well, Daniel replied, ready for the question, "for starters, you, Maggie and I friend him, and we can talk about him to our real friends and see how many of them check him out. We also get Leonard to friend the University of Chicago, Thunderbird, a bunch of professional financial groups, hell, any number of organizations that relate to what he does for a living. We'll get him set up on LinkedIn and he can tie into all kinds of groups and discussions there"

Jess listened closely, paused and said, "Oh my God, I see where you're going here. We can make him this out-in-front social media guy who has his hands in everything."

"Exactly," Daniel answered. "We'll get him to friend local and national media people, politicians, shit even McDonalds and Burger King. Maggie says there's no limit to how many people Leonard can connect to once we set things in motion."

Jess was smiling as Daniel went on about two becoming four becoming eight, how things will grow exponentially.

As Daniel sipped the last bit of his second vodka tonic, Jess said, "I just thought of something that might be a problem. Leonard needs a face."

Daniel looked at him and nodded. "Yeah, I thought of that too and I'm not sure what to do."

Jess' expression slowly turned from serious to a smile. "Oh wow, I just got an idea," he said, seemingly lost in thought.

Daniel waited a moment then said, "So tell me your big idea."

Jess held up both hands and said, "Let's hold off until tomorrow. I want to make sure I can pull this off."

"Pull what off?"

"Getting a photograph of Leonard Allen Paduszka," Jess answered.

Tuesday May 22nd

Jess parked his car in his usual spot in the lot behind Midwest Reprographics. He had made sure he got to the lot earlier than necessary. It was 7:02 AM and he didn't have to be at his desk until 8:30. Midwest was employee-owned, very progressive with their approach to employee relations and, all in all, a good place to work. Jess didn't make as much money as he could elsewhere, but he liked the easygoing pace of the office and the people were mellow and friendly. Until he found his wealthy widow he had no plans to leave.

He sat in the car, sipping a convenience store coffee, NPR on the radio and the morning sun shining in the side window. "Come on Sid," he muttered softly, "where are you?" He looked back and forth across the parking lot and down the service alley that linked it to the street. Midwest was smack in the middle of a light industrial area of town, less than two blocks from the City Mission homeless shelter and a Salvation Army thrift store.

Both places attracted a colorful and interesting group of people to the neighborhood. One morning last March while Jess was getting out of his car, he saw a thin, gray haired man, shabbily dressed but very clean, carrying a dark blue backpack. Despite his lot in life he had a posture and a proud bearing that were hard to miss. Jess had said hello to the man, who stopped to talk to him about the previous night's ice storm. Jess was struck by the man's clear, piercing blue eyes and his deeply tanned skin that could only come from years spent outdoors and on the street. His voice was raspy, every syllable of every word sounded like it was rubbing against sandpaper, and he didn't always finish his sentences. Jess found the man strangely captivating. Jess had a hunch that, despite the way he talked, he was a lot smarter than people gave him credit for. He said his name was Sid, extended his hand and as Jess shook it, he said, "Sid, it's very nice to meet you." And he meant it.

After that first, cold morning encounter he saw Sid once or twice a week. Jess could always tell when Sid had spent the night at the homeless shelter because he would be freshly shaven and his clothes would be noticeably cleaner. Jess made several attempts to find out more about Sid's past but could never get him to say much. One thing he knew was that Sid made it a point to find a discarded newspaper, someplace, every day because, as he said, "You have to know what's going on . . . around you so you can . . . be ready for it." Jess couldn't tell if the comment came from Sid's interest in the world or his paranoia from living on the streets, or just because it was a way to fill his time. Sid never asked Jess for money, but more than once Jess offered him some. Sid would always hesitate and look down, embarrassed, before finally looking him in the eye, accepting it with a gracious smile and a sincere thank you. The two men had forged a comfortable and respectful acquaintance.

Jess looked at the clock on the dashboard; 7:46 AM, and he'd have to head in the back door soon. He caught some movement out of the corner of his eye, turned and saw Sid walking slowly toward him. Jess opened the car door, climbed out and called, "Mornin' Sid, how are you?"

Sid smiled and said, "Oh, pretty good . . . I guess."

Jess said, "Actually man, I've been sitting here waiting and hoping I'd run into you."

Sid looked at him, puzzled. "What for?" he asked.

"Well, I need a favor and I thought you'd be just the guy who could help me."

"Me?" Sid asked, "really?"

"Yeah, I've got this little project here at the office. I need to get a couple of pictures of a guy and he has to be in his forties like you. All the guys in the office are too young so they asked me to find someone." Sid still had the puzzled look on his face and before he could say anything more, Jess said, "It's really important, Sid, and I can pay you fifty bucks for doing it."

Sid's face lit up. "Sure Jess, I'll do it. Just tell me . . . what you want me to do and . . . I'll do it."

This was the part Jess hadn't completely worked out. All he knew was he needed multiple photos of a man from different angles, some outdoors and some indoors. The timing was perfect because the morning was bright and from what Jess could tell, Sid had shaved and showered and was wearing a clean tee-shirt. Jess reached back into his car and took out a black camera bag, unzipped it and pulled out his digital camera. Sid looked at it. "Oh, so you mean like . . . right now."

"Yeah," Jess answered, "I have a tight deadline."

Sid nodded and said, "Okay."

For the next twenty minutes Jess had Sid stand and face in different directions, some with the sun in his face, some in shadow, some standing, some walking and even some waving. In some shots he asked Sid to smile, laugh, look serious or just look into the camera. They went inside the rear entrance vestibule of Midwest so Jess could get some shots in artificial light. In two shots Sid sat in a chair. In one he gazed out the window and in another he stood, pretending to talk into the wall-mounted security phone. By 8:24 AM, when Jess looked at the read-out of his camera it said he had taken forty-seven photographs.

"Okay, I think that should do it Sid. I really appreciate your help here." Jess reached for his wallet and took out two twenties and a ten and handed them to Sid. Jess could tell by the look on Sid's face it was probably more money than he had held in his hands in a very long time.

Sid looked at Jess, the tears in his deep, blue eyes noticeable, and said, "Jess . . . thank you. I would have helped you out . . . for free."

Jess felt a lump in his throat. Sid had no idea how Jess planned to use the photos. He had just trusted him and said yes.

Jess smiled and said, "You earned it Sid, you earned it." The proud smile on Sid's face stayed on Jess' mind for the rest of the day.

Wednesday May 23rd

When Daniel opened the front door and saw the huge grin on Jess' face he couldn't help but smile too. "Okay," Daniel asked, a bit of suspicion in his tone, "What's the big surprise you just had to drive over and deliver in person?"

Maggie walked into the foyer just as Jess entered. "Hey Maggs, how are you?" he asked.

Maggie knew that Jess had announced having a surprise for them and shared Daniel's curious suspicion. "Hi Jess," she said, "I'm fine, come on into the kitchen, I was just pouring us some wine."

Jess followed them into the kitchen and asked, "Can one of you get a laptop and set it up?"

Maggie left the room and returned with her computer, set it on the counter in front of Jess and asked, "Okay, what's the big surprise?"

Jess' grin was even wider. He reached into the pocket of his jeans, pulled out a thumb drive and said, "Maggs, Daniel, plug this in and watch."

She clicked the drive into her USB port and she and Daniel kept their eyes on the screen as Jess stood there quietly, still grinning. After waiting a minute or so for the download to finish, a long list of jpeg images appeared on the screen. Daniel looked at Jess and before he could say anything, Jess said, "Boys and girls, meet Leonard Paduszka."

Maggie sat in front of the keyboard, looked up at Jess, then clicked on the first image file. Jess watched their faces as Sid's first photo flashed on to the screen.

Daniel looked at Jess. "Who is this?" Jess answered,

"Its Leonard Paduszka."

"Come on, man, I mean who is it really?"

"It's a guy named Sid. He's homeless. I met him a few months ago near the homeless shelter down the street from my office."

Maggie looked up at Daniel, then at Jess. "This thing is suddenly getting weird. Why do we need pictures?" Jess and Daniel looked at each other, both knowing the answer to her question.

Daniel said to her, "Honey, think about it. Leonard needs a Facebook image, it's called FACE book. He needs it for LinkedIn too. He has to be as real and human as we can make him. You can't be real without a face for people to see and have a feeling about."

Jess added, "And from what Sid has told me, he has no family or friends, so there's no one who would come across him on the internet. He's a man without a face as far as the rest of the world is concerned Hell, whoever looks closely at a homeless person when it's so damn easy to look the other way?"

Maggie shook her head. "I know I agreed to help you with this little project, but all of a sudden a real person is involved, not just someone you made up."

Maggie clicked on the next image, then slowly went down the list of photos of Sid, or more correctly, of Leonard Allen Paduszka.

As she and Daniel looked at them, Jess added narrative. "I wanted to get him outdoors and indoors. I like that one because he looks serious, and look, check out that one, he has a great smile when you get him going. That one's nice because of the way he's squinting in the sun."

By the time they got to image twenty-one Daniel couldn't stay silent any longer. "Okay, your friend Sid looks like he meets the demographic. He looks like a normal middle-aged guy." But, let's face it, the settings for the photos look like what they are, a fucking parking lot, an alley full of dumpsters and a building that's not exactly from Manhattan."

Jess was ready for the comment and quickly responded, "Come on, man, I know that, but that's where you come in Maggie." She looked at Jess, waiting for the rest of his explanation. "I tried to get Sid, I mean Leonard, in every kind of pose and expression, indoors and out. Maggs, I know how good you are with PhotoShop and In Design, I saw that scrapbook you made for your friend's wedding shower and the bachelorette party. My God, those crazy pictures looked so real I gotta believe somebody got into trouble over them."

Maggie nodded, but before she could say anything Daniel said, "Yeah, Maggie knows the software, but what do you think she's going to do with these pictures?

Jess poured himself a glass of wine because Maggie was too focused on Sid's photos to be the proper bartender. "I figure that these pictures show Leonard, at least his face, in enough poses and directions and expressions to Photo Shop into a whole bunch of backgrounds." Daniel and Maggie were looking at the cascading images of Sid as Jess continued. "Maggie, there are enough faces and poses there to make it look like Leonard is into all kinds of stuff, all kinds of hobbies and work and business shit."

Maggie stopped her clicking down the list of images and said, "So let me get this straight, these jpegs are just to use with backgrounds and other images. You want me to put your friend Sid . . ."

"Whoa," Jess interrupted, "wait a minute don't think Sid, think Leonard, Leonard Paduszka."

"Okay," Maggie continued, "Leonard. You want me to put these faces and images into pictures that will make him look like a real person." Daniel looked at Jess. Jess looked back at him, then at Maggie. There was a moment of silence then Maggie grinned and said, "Oh my God, I love it!"

Jess noticed Daniel looking at him with the same suspicious look on his face. Daniel asked, "How did you talk this guy into posing?"

Jess hesitated. "Yeah, I guess I forgot to tell you. I gave him fifty bucks."

Daniel was clearly irritated and said, "I thought we agreed no more expenses unless we talked about it."

"Well," Jess answered, "I just figured it was too good of a chance to pass up, and I figured you would have done the same thing."

Daniel turned and walked to the refrigerator. "Geez, I'm into this thing for a hundred bucks already," he muttered.

"And by the way," Jess said, "it's like I told you, this man, Sid, has no family and, to be honest, he doesn't seem too curious about the whole thing I thought that made him the perfect choice." Daniel nodded his agreement.

For the next hour and a half, the three partners in fantasy looked through the photographs of Sid. Daniel scrawled their ideas on a legal pad as they shouted out comments on the ways they could depict all sorts of things that would bring Leonard to life. This picture could be cropped, and with minor tweaks could be Leonard's Facebook picture. Here was another picture that Maggie could make look like Leonard was on a golf course. Here was one where she could give him a commanding presence sitting behind a desk. Another one would be easy to manipulate and made to look like Leonard was in front of a crowd making a speech. Jess looked at Daniel, then at Maggie. They were totally engrossed in putting Leonard into real-world context. Jess stood there smiling. The pride he felt from his original idea was tempered by recollection of that morning's activity with Sid, the man's easy smile, his willingness to go along with the whole thing, his enthusiasm to do whatever Jess asked. Jess knew he had to make sure nothing happened with Leonard that could lead to trouble for Sid.

By the time Daniel's two bottles of wine were empty, the three of them had each committed to putting in some amount of time every day to make Leonard come alive. Maggie had created the Facebook photo and, with the help of photographs she found on a public domain clip-art website, she created three fake photographs of Leonard in various activities. Their list of images to complete included Leonard at a black-tie political gathering, Leonard posing with a group of fellow skiers in Vail and Leonard with his arms around two beautiful women in swimsuits at a beachside bar. "Geez," Jess said, laughing, "Leonard has a better life than I do."

Thursday May 24th

Daniel spent the morning with John Sherman working on a plan to convince Archie Baggins to invest in the franchises they had told him about. They had scheduled a meeting with him for Monday and Daniel figured he'd be finalizing some of the details all through the weekend. He knew that Sherman had brought him into the quest because of his reputation for closing this kind of deal. He worked hard and it hadn't been easy, but he had come up with an idea to land Baggins' money without fudging the numbers or lying about sales volumes like Jess had suggested. As he worked, Daniel's mind was never far from Leonard Paduszka. He still wasn't sure how he could or would use this newly created man for business purposes, but for now, he was having fun watching his little project take flight.

By the end of the workday Daniel was mentally drained and ready to do anything that didn't involve Archie Baggins. His personal dislike for the man was shared by John Sherman, and it only made it harder to work on pursuing his account. Daniel sent Maggie a quick text message saying he was going to stay at John's office an extra hour then head for home. She answered with a message saying she'd pick up Chinese on her way home so she'd have more time to work on some ideas for Leonard.

Wednesday June 6th

Daniel sat back in his beat up old recliner chair and looked over the spreadsheet he had printed out. Since his job required him to create mountains of forms and paperwork, he figured "why not be just as organized with the *Leonard Paduszka Project?*" He had put together a detailed view of the individual tasks that he, Jess and Maggie had been assigned, and a tracking calendar to chart their progress. As he read through the lines and columns he couldn't help but think how creating a person was turning out to be an incredibly detailed undertaking.

The first group of tasks on the spreadsheet was shaded in green and included the things that he had volunteered to do. He had opened an e-mail account on Yahoo with the name *chicagoleonard47*. Then he used that address and created an identity for Leonard on LinkedIn. Leonard's profile included a detailed back story, work history, personal information and Leonard's interests. Most of it was based on Daniel's own imagination and dreams. Maggie had created a realistic head shot of Leonard for the profile, using Sid's smiling face and the torso of a well-dressed businessman. And to give Leonard a real voice, Daniel created a blog for him, so Daniel a.k.a. Leonard's passion for business and politics could be expressed. Daniel's interest in writing was given a venue with the blog, which he had named *Don't Just Stand There*. It was already taking up much of his free time and even his coffee breaks during the workday, but the satisfaction and opportunity to vent more than made up for it.

The next assignments on the spreadsheet were shaded yellow and were Jess' responsibilities. He had taken the birth certificate and Social Security card that Daniel had found among his late uncle's memorabilia, and given them to his friend at Midwestern Reprographics. In just two days, working after business hours, the man created two perfect looking documents. For all intents and purposes, Leonard Allen Paduszka was now a legal, living and breathing citizen of the United States. There still was no plan to use those documents, but just in case, they were ready. Jess was also responsible for getting Leonard's name in front of people in a much more random way. He used the name *Leonard Paduszka, Chicago,* and sent dozens of comments to the editorial pages of the Chicago Tribune, Sun Times and even the Daily Herald. He sent responses and comments on news articles on the CNN, Fox News and MSNBC websites and even responses to music postings on You Tube. Anyone reading the comments would think that Leonard was a bright, thoughtful person, articulate, with liberal political leanings and a passion for jazz.

Maggie's items were shaded in blue and were at the core of everything that would happen as their project moved ahead. Her work in Photo Shop was masterful, and she had totally transformed Sid into a successful, outspoken and gregarious man named Leonard. She created sixteen photographs that portrayed his many sides; businessman, athlete, community volunteer and all around solid citizen. She still had the other thirty-one photographs that Jess had taken of Sid, and she agreed with Daniel and Jess' plan to hold off using them for now. That way they would have a bank of images to use for specific situations that might arise in the future. In addition to the photographs, Maggie created a Facebook page and opened Twitter and Instagram accounts for Leonard. She, Daniel and

Jess were his first three friends and they planned to carry on conversations with him on their own accounts to make his name more familiar to other people. The last line on her list of tasks was one that she thought of on her own and informed Daniel of just in time for him to add it to the spreadsheet. She registered Leonard on E-Harmony as a successful, divorced man looking for friendship first and a possible romance later. It appeared that Leonard Paduszka was also a romantic.

Saturday June 23rd

Daniel and Jess walked through the gate near the putting green and headed to Jess' car. Their two and a half hours of work on the driving range and then honing their putting skills seemed like a great way to unwind and put the work week behind them. They finished putting their clubs into the trunk and Jess asked, "Feel like a beer?"

"Sure," Daniel answered then added, "and I assume you really mean you want a beer and not just go on another reconnaissance mission for an available rich woman."

"Man that hurts," Jess replied in mock indignation, "for you to think I could be that fucking shallow in my search for true love . . . well, it just hurts me."

Daniel looked at him and said, "Wow, you actually said that with a straight face."

They took their usual seats at the grill room bar and ordered their beer. Daniel told Jess how his proposal to Archie Baggins was hand delivered on Friday and he and John were hoping to hear back from the little jerk by Monday or Tuesday. Jess told Daniel about a new print account he had locked up and how the deal would probably mean a salary bump for him. Both men were feeling relaxed and upbeat, and with the help of their beer, the conversation turned to things other than their jobs, and eventually, to the Leonard project.

"Man, I don't know about you, but all of the things I'm doing for Leonard are starting to catch fire," Daniel said.

Jess sipped his beer and nodded. "Yeah, me too, it's like he's been around for years instead of, what's it been, two weeks?"

"Actually less than that," Daniel answered, "it's kind of scary when you think about it."

Jess smiled smugly and said, "Yeah, every once in a while I get a good idea and I guess this was one of them." He took a long slow sip of his beer and said, "Oh, by the way, I saw Sid yesterday."

"How's he doing?" Daniel asked. "Oh, about the same, every time I see him he seems happy, or at least not desperate, and he's definitely a talker. Sometimes I can't get him to stop."

"Does he ever ask you about the pictures you took of him?"

"Nope, not once, I'm not even sure he remembers that I took them."

Over Jess' shoulder Daniel noticed an attractive brunette in tennis attire walking into the room. She was alone and Daniel was tempted to point her out to Jess but he held back. He was enjoying the beer and the conversation and didn't want to add any distractions.

"So when are you gonna start using Leonard to help your business?" Jess asked.

"I'm not sure, and I'm still trying to figure out how I can use him, but I have another idea."

Before Daniel could say more Jess turned and noticed the brunette. "Whoa, where'd she come from?"

Daniel knew right then there was no point in trying to continue the conversation. Jess had obviously changed his focus from Leonard to the attractive tennis player, and there was little hope of getting him back until he decided it was time. The woman sat down at a table not far from where Daniel and Jess were sitting, and when she glanced in their direction, Jess smiled and nodded to her. She returned his smile with one of her own and it was dazzling. Jess turned to Daniel and asked, "Very nice, what do you think, 40, 45?"

"Yeah, that sounds about right," Daniel answered, "and I don't see a ring on her hand."

Jess grinned. "She's gorgeous."

Daniel made an attempt to restart their conversation about Leonard, but after a few minutes he gave up. Talking to the side of Jess' face and getting one or two word responses made it clear that conversation was not going to be productive for the rest of the day.

Without saying a word, Jess stood up and walked over to the woman. Daniel noticed her smile and how she seemed pleased by Jess' attention. When Jess sat down at her table, Daniel knew his plans with his friend were about to change. He took out his cellphone and called Maggie. After a moment he said, "Hi babe, looks like Jess has fallen in love again, can you pick me up?" As he listened to Maggie he looked over at Jess, then said quietly into the phone, "I'm looking right at him and judging by the look on his face, there's no way I should interrupt him." He listened to Maggie's lengthy reply, and then said, "Okay, I'll be out front under the portico, see you in twenty. Thanks babe." Daniel finished his beer and laid a ten dollar bill on the bar. Before he left he sent Jess a text message that said, "Maggie's on her way, good luck big fella."

Sunday June 24th

Having an entire day alone with Maggie was something Daniel hadn't enjoyed in a long time. Since she had moved in with him it seemed that both their lives got busier, and *couple-time* was a rare commodity. She had been a good sport about giving up her free time to help Daniel create Leonard, and she, more than Daniel or Jess, was most responsible for the success of their plan. But as enthusiastic and hard working as she had been on the project, Daniel still knew she was concerned about avoiding anything that could be called illegal.

After a leisurely hour-long stint of coffee and newspaper on the patio they split a short list of housekeeping chores, then showered, dressed and moved into the kitchen. Maggie sat at the counter finishing a list of groceries to pick up while Daniel went into the study. A few minutes later he returned and sat down with a large sheet of paper that caught Maggie's eye. "What's that?" she asked.

Daniel turned the paper toward her then quickly flipped it back to read it again. "It's the Leonard spreadsheet. I updated it on Friday and haven't had a chance to really look it over."

"You know," she replied, "I would love a whole day without Leonard, it's like he's moved in with us."

"Oh, I'm sorry honey," Daniel said as he put the spreadsheet aside, "you're right. We all have spent too much time with this little project."

Despite her comment, Maggie's curiosity was as strong as Daniel's, and after a minute or so she picked up the spreadsheet and started to read it. After about a minute, she laid it back down and said, "Oh my God, this thing has gotten huge."

Daniel couldn't help but smile. "I know," he said with the pride of a new father, "our little boy is growing up."

Maggie let out an unrestrained laugh and asked, "Does that mean I'm his mother?"

They gave up on their resistance to dwelling on the project and for the next twenty minutes they talked about Leonard. He had already built a list of seventy-four friends on Facebook and had been actively involved there with four groups. He tweeted on a daily basis to over two-hundred contacts, and *Don't Just Stand There* was raising eyebrows both locally and nationally.

Following Daniel's writing style, Jess was making sure that Leonard sent numerous comments, stridently liberal, to the newspapers and news channel websites. He expanded the list to include the New York Times, Wall Street Journal and Washington Post. Leonard/Jess wrote the letters in a way that was guaranteed to stir the emotions of people at both ends of the political spectrum. Jess had told Daniel how Leonard had given him a voice that he had never used before, and also assured him that he cleaned up his language whenever he spoke as Leonard. Jess had always seemed to enjoy saying things that would piss off somebody, and now Leonard was helping him do it on a much broader scale. The responses to Leonard's comments were getting stronger and more frequent. Leonard Paduszka was definitely making a name for himself.

Daniel's recent activity on the project had been sporadic, his input based on the time he had available when he wasn't consulting on four new franchise accounts. His hard work on the proposal with John had convinced Baggins to invest, and Franchise Holdings was in a position to make a lot of money. That fact wasn't lost on John Sherman, who signed a contract with Daniel to assist on three new major accounts. It was a reward for Daniel's hard work and a very nice fee. Daniel was flattered and grateful for the business but it made it hard to keep up with his share of Project Leonard. He worked extra hours trying to clear some time but that was only a slight improvement. He still didn't seem to have enough time for Maggie, let alone Leonard. That fact bothered him but he didn't know how to change it.

Monday June 25th

Taking advantage of a cancelled appointment with a prospective franchisee, Daniel spent a few minutes looking through a long list of e-mail messages to ChicagoLeonard47. Among them was one with the tagline *Opportunity, Please Contact Me.* Daniel opened the message and read it, then read it again. It was from the news editor of the Sun-Times and he wanted to talk with Leonard about adding *Don't Just Stand There* to the newspaper's online editorial content. Daniel grinned smugly as he read the lengthy message a third time. When he got back to his desk he used Leonard's e-mail account to send messages to Maggie and Jess to tell them the news, and he asked them for their ideas on what to do. After several rounds of back and forth messages they agreed to meet after work at *Rockford's* to talk about it.

Jess had already stationed himself in the corner booth when Daniel and Maggie arrived at almost the same time. Daniel carried the omnipresent yellow file folder and Maggie had her laptop. Jess was empty handed. "Hey," Jess said, "I waited to order until you got here."

Daniel smiled and said sarcastically, "Your restraint is impressive." Jess slid to the right so Daniel and Maggie could sit together. "Hey," Daniel said to Jess, "you never told me how things went with the tennis player on Saturday."

Jess smiled and looked down, then said, "Let's talk about that later."

By the time Maggie's laptop was set up and the contents of the file folder were spread out a young server named Josh showed up to take their drink order. After he walked away and was out of ear shot, Jess said, "So, this is exciting, man, you're finally ready to put Leonard to work."

Before Daniel could say anything Maggie interrupted, "Yeah, honey, it sounds like this little project finally has a purpose."

"Well," he answered, "the original plan was for Leonard to be an expert on franchising and reading the dining trends of America but it's obviously turned into something else.

"Point taken," Jess interrupted, "tomorrow Leonard will comment on the uptick in pork consumption in the American diet."

"Where did you hear that?" Maggie wondered.

"On a blog from the American Pork Council, and if you can't trust a pig farmer who can you trust?"

Daniel took two pages from the stack of paperwork he'd removed from the yellow folder and handed one page each to Maggie and Jess. "Okay, this is just a quick overview, it's all I had time to put together this afternoon, but I think it gives you the basic idea."

The three of them took a moment to read the outline and finally Maggie looked at Daniel and said, "I like it, honey, it's a wonderful idea."

"Yeah," Jess added, "I agree, very good, I like the neighborhood focus instead of going big with it."

Daniel's plan was to use *Don't Just Stand There* to create a program called *Close to Home,* where individual business owners defined the boundaries of their neighborhood, the area where their regular customers lived or worked. Within those specific boundaries the businesses would tap into multiple opportunities to work with neighborhood residents and local politicians. They would prioritize issues, set goals and develop a political action plan, all from a neighborhood perspective. Nothing outside of their immediate neighborhood would be allowed to interfere with the mission. Local councilmen and councilwomen would be held accountable by the people who lived on their street, sold them their groceries and mowed their lawns. They would have nowhere to run and nowhere to hide.

Maggie looked at Daniel and said, "Honey, I'm really proud of you, this is a wonderful idea, but what about the blog itself, are you still going to have time to write it?"

"Yeah, I guess I'll have to make the time."

Jess added, "And you'll still have to make time to write all those things that piss off so many people?"

Daniel laughed, "That's still your department man, you have such a knack for it." Daniel went on," You saw in the e-mail that they want a commitment from Leonard by the end of the week, and they have a schedule already put together for his posts.

Jess re-read Daniel's outline and said, "I see here at the bottom that Leonard will be the face of this program. Tell me how that works."

"Well," Daniel started, "we've already put Leonard out there as a successful businessman who loves politics and community service stuff, right?"

Maggie interjected, "That seems to be what all of his Facebook friends think." "And his contacts on LinkedIn too," Daniel added. "Leonard has become an authority on ways that businesses and communities should work together, and there are hundreds and hundreds of people who know that on-line. Now we bring all of that into the real world. I'll present this idea to the newspaper as if it's coming from Leonard. Jess sat silently, listening to Daniel and Maggie. Daniel noticed the troubled look on his face. "What's the matter Jess?"

Jess took a long, slow drink of his beer then answered, "I'm just sitting here thinking about Sid and how this all might affect him. I get that this is a great idea and all the neighborhood rah-rah shit will help people, but what about Sid's face?"

"What do you mean, his face?" Daniel asked.

"I mean, to all of those people online Sid doesn't exist. He's a real man who doesn't exist and Leonard is a fake man who does exist, and they share a face."

Maggie joined in with," And you think that something bad can happen to Sid because of it."

"I'm not saying that exactly, but stop and think about it. Leonard will finally shows up someplace that isn't online, like the newspaper. All of a sudden average people see him. And average people see Sid too."

Daniel hesitated then looked over at Maggie. She shrugged and said, "He's got a point."

"Nah, I don't think we have to worry about that," Daniel replied, his voice tinged with frustration, "From everything you've told us about Sid he spends most of his time on the streets and hangs at the shelter once in a while. It's not just the fact that almost nobody ever sees him, it's also that nobody pays attention to him. When most people encounter a homeless person they look the other way."

Jess waited for Daniel to finish then replied, "I don't disagree with anything you said, it's just that this suddenly has the potential to go south on us if anyone ever saw the link between Sid and Leonard."

Maggie nodded and said, "I agree with you Jess, but it seems like the odds are a million to one that anyone who might have seen Leonard's face would ever see Sid's too."

"Yeah, man," Daniel added, "besides you."

Friday June 29th

Daniel sat nervously at his desk in his cozy home office, the contents of the yellow folder spread out in front of him. After months of existing only online, Leonard Allen Paduszka was about to make his first phone call. After two days of e-mail exchanges full of attachments, the deal to bring *Don't Just Stand There* into the Sun-Times blogosphere was ready to go. The people at the paper had requested a personal meeting but Daniel a.k.a. Leonard made up the excuse that he was on vacation in Canada, and the deal would have to happen via mail and e-mail. He promised he would meet with them when he got back, but also promised that the first three installments of the blog would be sent long before then. That seemed to satisfy the newspaper. Now, for the first time in his short life, Leonard was going to speak.

Daniel punched the editor's number into his cellphone, leaned back in his chair and waited. After the fifth ring Daniel was ready to hang up, but finally a man answered, "Doug Stewart here."

Daniel took a breath and said, "Mr. Stewart . . . Doug, it's Leonard Paduszka."

"Oh, how are you Leonard, nice to finally speak with you."

"Yeah, same here," Daniel said, "I have a few minutes here before I have to tee-off and I wanted to make sure we had a chance to talk."

"Well, thanks, I appreciate it. Where are you?"

"I'm in British Columbia, a place called Emerald Lake Lodge."

"Yeah, I've heard that place is incredible, great scenery, great food . . . everything."

"Yep, it's all of that . . . kind of pricey though."

Stewart chuckled, "That's what happens, they get you there with a great deal offer then charge you extra for every little thing."

There was a pause then Daniel asked, "So did you have a chance to look over the contract and my comments?"

"Yes I did," Stewart replied, "and everything looks good. I'm sorry if it feels like we're pressuring you but we already have the rollout ads ready for print and we'll need those first three posts right away."

"No problem Doug," Daniel answered, "The first one's done and I'll wrap up number two tonight. You'll have number three in a few days after I get back."

Stewart said, "And if you just follow the upload instructions that Dianne sent to you there shouldn't be any problems."

"Will do," Daniel said, and then added, "Hey Doug, I have to run. I'll definitely call you when I'm back in town."

"Thanks Leonard, I appreciate the call, enjoy the rest of your trip."

Daniel laid his cellphone on his desk and thought, "Man that was the weirdest phone call I ever made in my life." He refolded the brochure for Emerald Lake Lodge that Maggie had given him when they were talking about a fall vacation. "Geez," he thought as he stuffed the papers back into the yellow folder, "I wonder how long Leonard can go without actually meeting someone."

Sunday July 1st

Daniel stood at the kitchen counter, filling two cups with coffee while Maggie separated the advertising supplements from the rest of the newspaper.

"Damn," she complained, "all these tabloids and circulars advertising nothing but crap. Look how many there are."

"Well," Daniel replied sarcastically, "the Fourth of July is in a few days and what better way to express your love of country than by buying wieners and plastic lawn chairs?"

Maggie completed her sorting and they walked out to the patio. They had no sooner settled into their chairs when Maggie said, "Hey, hey, hey," look at this." She folded back a section of the paper and handed it to Daniel. He saw the quarter-page ad for *Don't Just Stand There,* the picture of Leonard/Sid, neatly dressed in a business suit, featured prominently on the left side, and a large, bold heading that read "Starting Sunday July 8th!"

Daniel turned to Maggie and smiled, "Our little boy has finally found gainful employment."

Maggie laughed and said, "That's right, I forgot that he's actually going to get paid for this thing."

Daniel nodded and said, "I suggest we split it evenly three ways, what do you think?"

Maggie started to nod and then said, "Uh oh, we have a problem."

"What's that?"

"They'll be making out checks to Leonard Paduszka, so who's going to cash them?"

Daniel tossed the section of newspaper on to the table and said, "I thought about that when they sent me the contract. One of the options is a direct deposit, so I signed Leonard's name and gave their accounting department my account number. I stopped at the bank on the way home on Friday and added Leonard's name to the account."

Maggie said, "Oh, I thought you could only do that in person."

"So did I," Daniel said, "but only if he'll be writing checks on the account."

Maggie smiled, "So you're just going to take our boy's money and not give him any of it."

"Yeah, I'm a selfish SOB."

Tuesday July 3rd

Jess gathered up the files from his desk and stuffed them into the pouch of his laptop bag. It was nearly noon and he had already worked longer than he had planned. The day was considered a floating holiday at Midwest Reprographics and most of the staff had stayed home, but his new account added to his normal duties and he was still trying to get into a rhythm with his expanded workload. He looked at his watch and thought, "I hope I get somewhere with that tennis player because this working on holidays shit really sucks."

He locked the rear door and headed to his car and just as he reached it a raspy voice said, "Hey Jess." He turned and saw Sid walking toward him, his dark blue backpack slung over his shoulder. His usual smile was missing.

"Hi Sid, how are you?"

"Well," Sid answered slowly, "I don't know . . . okay I guess." He was looking down and seemed troubled.

"Anything wrong?" Jess asked.

Sid reached into a pocket of his backpack and pulled out a newspaper. He fumbled with it, obviously trying to find something among the wrinkled pages and Jess already had a feeling he knew what was coming. Finally Sid folded back a page and then folded it again in half. He handed it to Jess. "Is this me?" he asked.

Jess saw the ad for *Don't Just Stand There* with Sid's photograph. Before Jess could answer Sid said, "I don't think it's me 'cause I don't have a nice suit like that . . . or a tie." He was visibly confused and, Jess thought, a little bit upset too.

"Man," Jess thought, "what do I say to this poor guy?"

Sid kept looking at the picture in the newspaper, shaking his head and saying, "I don't think that's me 'cause I don't have a nice suit like that . . . or a tie."

Jess looked at him for a moment then opened his car door, laid his bag on the passenger seat, then closed and locked the door. "Hey Sid, I was thinking of going over to *Perino's* for lunch, want to join me?"

Sid looked at him and replied, "Oh I don't think I have enough money . . . for that, Jess."

"No, no, it's my treat, come on."

The two men walked across the parking lot, through the service alley, then jaywalked across the street to the restaurant. Sid didn't say a word until they sat down in a booth along the front window. "Didn't . . . you take some pictures . . . of me?" he asked.

Jess waited a moment while Sid carefully set his backpack on the seat beside him. "Yes, Sid, remember a couple of months ago? You let me take some pictures of you and I paid you fifty dollars."

Sid nodded, seeming to remember. Before Jess could continue a woman in a red and white striped blouse and black slacks stopped at their table. "Are you gentlemen here for lunch?" she asked, looking at Sid with a suspicious expression.

"Yes we are," Jess answered, and please give me the check. "What looks good to you Sid?" Sid picked up a menu and read through it. Jess wondered how long it had been since the man had eaten a restaurant meal.

The waitress seemed impatient as Sid stared at the menu, and Jess gave her his own order first to give Sid a little more time. Finally Sid laid the menu on the table and said, "I want a cheeseburger . . . please."

The waitress paused then asked, "Is that all?"

Seeing his confusion over her question, Jess asked, "How about some French fries, Sid? Their fries are really good here."

"Okay," Sid said quietly.

"And we'll each have the apple pie ala-mode for desert, you know, Fourth of July kind of stuff,." Jess added. The waitress gave Jess a weak smile, looked back at Sid and walked away. Jess looked over at his bedraggled companion, who seemed uncomfortable sitting there. Sid ran his weathered hands over the fork and spoon and looked around at the other diners, most of who were looking back at him.

"Hey Sid," Jess started, "I wanted to talk to you about the pictures, the ones I took of you, remember?" Sid nodded. "Well, remember how I told you I needed pictures of a guy with gray hair because all of the guys in the office were too young?" Sid nodded again. "Well, I used those pictures on a project with a couple of my friends. Like I said, we needed the face of a guy about your age, and the picture in the paper is one of the ones we used."

Sid reached down and pulled out the paper again and looked at it. "Jess, how come I'm wearing a suit . . . and a tie?"

"That's because the person in the ad had to look like a businessman so we put your face on another picture of a man in a suit."

Jess was hoping his explanation made sense but Sid still looked confused. "It says here I'm going to be . . . in the newspaper . . . every Sunday, what does that mean?"

"Sid, it just means that the same picture will be in the newspaper, just like the one you're looking at, every week. My friend Daniel is writing some stuff about business and we want to have your picture with it. It's what I paid you for."

Sid nodded and seemed to accept what Jess had said. He kept staring at his face in the ad as if he didn't yet make the connection with the fact that in the picture he was wearing a suit and tie. The waitress walked up to the table and set their plates in front of them without speaking, then walked away. "She's . . . not very friendly . . . is she?" Sid asked.

"Nope, kind of rude actually," Jess answered. Sid took the ketchup bottle and poured some on his cheeseburger, then poured some on the large basket of French fries in the middle of the table. Jess watched as the ketchup poured until it all but covered the entire basket. Sid noticed Jess watching him and suddenly stopped. "Oh gee, I'm sorry Jess, are . . . those your fries too?"

Jess smiled, "Nope, they're all yours Sid, enjoy."

By the time the waitress delivered two plates of apple pie ala mode Sid had finished his cheeseburger, pickle and the entire basket of fries. By the clock on the wall behind him, it took Sid less than two minutes to eat his desert, and Jess watched as he scraped every crumb of pie and drop of ice cream from the plate.

When he was finished he looked up at Jess, pushed away the plate and asked, "Jess . . . the picture, am I . . . famous now?"

Jess smiled and said, "Well Sid, I guess, in a way, you are."

Monday July 8th

Daniel rushed into his office, dropped the pile of paperwork from his two morning meetings on his already cluttered desk, and headed back out the door. He had promised Maggie he'd meet her for lunch, a rare treat since their offices were so far apart. A meeting with a court stenographer brought her within a block of the Franchise Holdings office and they were eager to take advantage of the timing. His desk phone rang but he decided to let voicemail pick up the call, and he hurried out the door. It was just over a block to Cilantro Café and Daniel got there in time to select a table on the patio. He saw Maggie walk in and he waved to get her attention. His cellphone rang just as Maggie sat down. "Daniel Warren," he said, holding his right hand over his ear to cover the crowd noise.

Maggie looked over the menu for a moment then she noticed the expression on Daniel's face. That, and the fact he wasn't saying anything made her put down the menu and try to figure out what was going on. Finally Daniel said, "Look Doug, I can explain the whole thing." There was another long stretch of silence from Daniel and his grim expression never changed. "No, there's no reason for you to worry about that," he said, leaning forward nervously, "no reason at all." Maggie tried to give him hand signals to get him to tell her who he was talking to. "Alright, I can be there in about an hour, will that work for you?" After another long pause Daniel said, "I know we can work this out," and hung up.

"What was all that?" Maggie asked.

Daniel shook his head. "I'm not exactly sure but it looks like we have a big problem with the blog."

"What kind of problem?"

A young woman came to the table and said, "My name is Courtney and I'll be your server today." Before she could go on Daniel snapped, "We need a few minutes." The woman looked uncomfortable, muttered, "Sure, okay," and walked away.

"Okay," Maggie insisted, "tell me what the heck is going on."

Daniel paused then said, "Well it looks like our friend, Jess' friend Sid has introduced himself to the people at the Sun-Times."

"Oh my God, what happened?" Maggie said with a gasp.

"Yeah, it looks like Jess found a homeless man who likes to read the newspaper. Sid went to the Sun-Times office with a copy of the ad with his picture and said he wanted to be paid for it. One thing led to another and he ended up in a face-to-face with Doug Stewart. Apparently Sid is sharper than Jess thought."

Maggie sat back in her chair, looking at Daniel. "This is not good," she said.

Daniel nodded. "It's more than not good, it's a disaster. The Sun-Times is a major newspaper and they hold their ethics up like a badge of honor. Stewart thinks I conned him, made up the whole thing to humiliate the paper."

Daniel saw their server timidly approaching the table and stood up. "I'm sorry," he said to her, "we have to leave." Maggie grabbed her purse from the empty chair beside her and walked out with Daniel. They moved off to the curb, hoping to find some small degree of privacy on a lunch-hour city sidewalk. "I'm going to meet with Doug Stewart and try to explain all of this. I'm not sure what Sid's angle is here but I think we can head off any more trouble."

"What about Jess?" Maggie asked, "don't you think you should let him in on this? Sid was his idea."

"Yeah, I'll call him on my way to the Sun-Times."

They started to walk to the parking garage where Maggie had left her car. "I'm scared, honey," she said.

Daniel took her hand in his and said, "Look, we haven't broken any law or done anything to hurt anyone. We invented a person but that person hasn't hurt anyone."

Maggie looked up at Daniel. "A man with a fake identity just asked a major newspaper for money for using a picture they thought was legitimate. It sounds like somebody is going to get hurt somehow."

Daniel walked Maggie to the entrance of the garage then hurried back to his office. He told his assistant that he wasn't feeling well and was going home for the rest of the day. The drive to the Sun-Times office was agonizingly long.

The muscular, young security guard at the lobby desk showed him where to sign in and, even though he was tempted to sarcastically sign Leonard's name, he signed his name Daniel Warren. After the guard called upstairs and got the okay to send Daniel up to Doug Stewart's office, he said to Daniel, "It's the 16th floor, they're waiting for you."

Daniel got on to the crowded elevator and when the doors opened on 16, a grim faced woman in a black business suit was waiting for him. "Are you Mr. Paduszka?" she asked without a trace of a smile.

"Well, that's my pen name so to speak. My name is Daniel Warren."

She turned around and with her back to him said, "Come this way." Daniel followed her down a long corridor and into a small conference room. "Please have a seat, Mr. Stewart and Mr. Long will be with you shortly." She left without another word.

Daniel sat at one end of the table, facing the door, and laid his leather notebook in front of him. After a few minutes two men walked in. "I'm Doug Stewart and this is our attorney, Ted Hill, and I assume you are Mr. Warren . . . or Mr. Paduszka. What shall we call you?" Neither man was smiling.

"I'm Daniel Warren."

Stewart was tall and stocky, with thinning gray hair and wire-framed glasses. He looked like a newspaper editor right out of a movie. Hill looked to be in his late forties, with reddish hair, horn rimmed glasses and a suit coat that obviously couldn't be buttoned around the man's ample stomach. The two men took seats on opposite sides of the table and turned toward Daniel. Doug Stewart started the conversation. "As I told you on the phone, this newspaper has a problem, and that means you also have a problem." Daniel nodded as Stewart continued. "A man named Sidney Kubek came to our offices this morning. He had a copy of last Sunday's edition with your blog, and he was clearly the man whose photograph is used next to your by-line."

Daniel felt like it was time for him to say something. "Yes, Sid is an acquaintance of my friend Jess."

"Does your friend Jess normally pal around with homeless people?"

"They don't pal around," Daniel said stiffly, "Jess met Sid because he hangs around the neighborhood where Jess works, and Jess just happens to have a big heart."

Ted Hill cleared his throat and said, "Mr. Kubek walked into our main lobby this morning and said he wanted to talk to the president. He kept going on and on that the newspaper was using his picture and he wanted be paid for it. At least six other people in the lobby heard what he said before security escorted him into Mr. Stewart's office. Mr. Kubek wasn't exactly clear on his link to the blog, but he kept saying over and over that he was famous."

Daniel looked over at Stewart, who had leaned back in his chair, crossed his arms and locked his gaze on to Daniel. "Mr. Warren," he started, "you write a blog, and I have to say it's a good one. So why in hell are you using a fake name and a fake picture? Is there some reason you don't want your real identity to be known?"

"Okay look," Daniel answered, "here's what's going on. I work in the world of franchising businesses, mainly fast food, the kind of places that feed you at the trough for very little money. I live and breathe statistics and demographics and trying to figure out what people want. My friends and I came up with this idea to create a person, or more like a persona. Create his back story and try to find a way to use this . . . this Leonard Paduszka, to speak for the consumers who spend their money at the businesses I work with." Stewart looked over at Hill while Daniel continued. "It was just meant to be an experiment in today's American culture, or as my friend called it, a slow walk through the trailer park." Stewart smiled slightly, probably without realizing it. "We used the internet, mainly social media and e-mail, to generate some buzz about Leonard. The man we created is meant to be in his late 40s and none of us is even 30 yet, so Jess got the idea to find someone who fit the age profile, and that led us to Sid."

Stewart sat totally still, his arms still crossed and his eyes locked on Daniel. He said, "So how does that explain your blog?"

"Well," Daniel answered, "when we really started putting together the details, we knew that Leonard had to have credibility, some gravitas, if we expected people to listen to him. That led us away from him being Joe Chilidog and eating at greasy spoons, and toward more of a serious, thoughtful person." Daniel looked at Stewart, trying to read his face but couldn't find any kind of clue as to what the man was feeling.

There was an uncomfortable silence, and then Ted Hill asked, "What did you hope to gain from all this deceit and fake identity stuff?"

Daniel hesitated. He and Jess and Maggie had been so busy building Leonard and writing the blog that they only had the haziest idea of exactly where they wanted it to go. "Well," he started slowly, "first of all, your choice of the word *deceit* is offensive. There has never been any intention of using Leonard or Sid or the blog for any kind of monetary gain or to hurt anyone." Hill kept his eyes on Daniel with no change of expression. "Fucking lawyers", Daniel thought, then continued. "None of us had a clue that Sid wanted to be paid for his photograph in the paper. We were surprised that he ever found out about the ad."

Stewart leaned forward and said, "Be that as it may, your fucking blog and your fucking homeless friend have made a big problem for this paper and we have to find a way out of it."

His words got Daniel's back up. "My *fucking homeless friend* is a human being and we paid him for his pictures to give him a little bit of help."

Ted Hill jumped back into the fray. "You should know that I'm here at the request of the newspaper to see what kind of legal action we might have to take against you."

Daniel leaned toward Hill, clearly angry and not backing down. "Legal action my ass, the paper hasn't been harmed in any way. I wrote two posts for a blog that you asked me to write. The posts were delivered and you printed them. As we sit here right now I have yet to be paid for them so you're not out any money. So explain to me what kind of legal action you have in mind."

Hill leaned back, obviously surprised by Daniel's stiff response. Stewart said, "You used a fake name for the blog"

"Call it my pen name," Daniel said.

"And you used the photograph of a . . . another person and passed it off as your own."

"No, I didn't. I paid a real person for a photo that depicts a fake person. Advertisers do that every day so how in the hell can you spin that as being something illegal?"

There was a pause as everyone seemed to realize the need to let things cool down. Finally Stewart said, "There's still the problem of a man who wants to be paid for his photograph, and we have no intention of paying him."

Daniel replied, "Mr. Stewart, Mr. Hill, you guys are looking at the wrong problem here. Giving a little bit of cash to a guy who's down on his luck is nothing compared to what will happen if word gets out that the Chicago Sun-Times didn't do any checking, and published the photo of a homeless guy and passed him off as an expert on small business."

Hill looked over at Stewart and nodded slightly. For a moment neither of the men replied to Daniel's comment, then Stewart said, "This paper operates with the highest ethical standards and this whole thing makes it look like we're either trying to fool the public, or at the very least, we don't properly vet the people who write for us."

Daniel leaned back in his chair and said, "All your paper has to do is the right thing, give this poor guy a couple of bucks, make him feel good about himself and send him on his way."

Stewart sat there staring at Daniel then looked over at Hill. Stewart asked him, "Ted, does that fix the problem from a legal point of view?"

"Well," Hill answered, "it makes Mr. Kubek go away but there's still the problem that the man who writes the blog doesn't seem to play things straight up."

Daniel glared at him. "Why, because I write from the viewpoint of a made-up person? For God sake, Pauline Phillips wrote for your freaking paper under the name Dear Abby."

Stewart sat almost slouched in his chair, looked at Hill then at Daniel. "We have some things to discuss internally," he said, "I'll have to get back to you later today, or maybe tomorrow."

Daniel clutched his notebook and stood up. Stewart didn't stand and Hill was busy writing something on a legal pad. "Thank you for your time," Daniel muttered and walked out.

Tuesday July 9th

Daniel was reviewing the financials of a small start-up bagel shop when his cellphone rang. He looked at the read-out on the screen and saw *Chicago Sun Times.* "Okay," he thought, "here we go." "Daniel Warren," he said, as strongly and unemotionally as possible.

"Mr. Warren . . . Daniel, this is Doug Stewart."

Daniel hesitated a moment then said, "Hi Doug, I was wondering when I'd hear from you."

After a short pause Stewart said, "We've been trying to figure out this whole damn thing and I want you to know it hasn't been easy.

"Yeah, it's been a strange situation from my end too," Daniel replied.

"Well," Stewart started slowly, "after Ted Hill and I had a chance to talk about what's at stake . . . and where this thing needs to go . . . we decided not to continue with your blog."

Daniel sat there for a moment, disappointed but not surprised, and said, "Okay, I had a hunch that's where this thing was heading."

"Believe me, Daniel, it wasn't an easy call to make. We like the way you write and what you have to say, but there are people on the Editorial Board that were uncomfortable with the whole idea of yours. A fictional person you created on the internet, writing and speaking on local business issues. They felt that your approach simply didn't pass our smell test, it was too far out."

Daniel waited a moment, trying to choose the right words then said, "I understand. I don't agree but I understand." He paused then asked, "And what about Sid?"

The silence on the other end of the phone told Daniel what he had expected all along. "Well," Stewart finally said, "after talking with Ted and the editorial folks, we decided that your friend is not due any compensation for a photograph we had nothing to do with."

Daniel tried to contain the anger that welled up inside him. "Nothing to do with, nothing to do with, except you printed it and sent it out twice, in tens of thousands of newspapers, and you put it up on your website that reaches who knows how many people."

There was another long stretch of silence then Stewart said, "I didn't expect you to understand our decision, but that's the way it is." After a short pause Stewart said, "Goodbye Daniel."

Wednesday July 10th

The modern, business-like offices of the Tribune were a sharp contrast from the elegant Neo-Gothic architecture of the building itself. Daniel sat nervously in the waiting area outside of David Bruce's office. Bruce was Editor-in-Chief of the Chicago Tribune and, after Daniel had called him and given him a brief history of the Leonard Paduszka project and its results, he asked Daniel to meet with him. Daniel's original intention was to find a new venue for his blog, but after he gave it more thought, he realized it was for reasons far beyond that. His meetings with the Sun-Times had angered him to a point where he knew he couldn't just leave everything at a dead end. He and Jess and Maggie had worked too hard for too long to just walk away from their creation.

A tall, thin impeccably dressed man walked into the waiting area and approached Daniel. He extended his hand and said," Daniel, I'm David Bruce, come on into my office." Daniel followed him into the largest and most perfectly designed office anyone could imagine. A corner office, twenty-five stories above Chicago, with views of the city that were breathtaking. "This is the freaking center of the newspaper universe," Daniel thought, as he sat down in front of Bruce's desk.

After the ritual offering of coffee, tea or water, Bruce said, "I asked a couple of people on my editorial staff to join us, they'll be here in a minute, but first I wanted to ask you why you called me, what you hope to gain from this. From what you told me on the phone this involves some kind of internet activity and a false identity situation."

Daniel was expecting Bruce's questions. "Well Mr. Bruce, to be blunt, my friends and I started a little project that got way out of hand, and it led us to a place that none of us expected. In the process a homeless man, a good man, was drawn into something he never asked for. I just want to see if there's anything you and I can do to fix things."

A short, stalky woman pushing a serving cart came into the office. "Thanks Rita," Bruce said, "just set things up over there on the conference table." The woman quietly went about placing pots of coffee and tea on the table, along with several plates of fresh cut fruit and pastries. While she was still laying out the cups and plates, a man and a woman walked in. "Let's move over there and I'll make the introductions," Bruce said. Daniel stood beside Bruce as he introduced him to Jacob Adelson and Rebecca Howland. Bruce referred to them as the backbone of the editorial team. The four of them made small talk as they poured their coffee and when they all finally sat down Bruce said, "Daniel, how about telling Jacob and Rebecca what you told me on the phone so we can see where this thing might lead us."

For the next few minutes Daniel retraced the details of the Leonard Paduszka project and the events of the last several months. He pulled out the yellow file folder from inside his notebook and gave them copies of the latest spreadsheet of activity. He had updated the information to include his meeting with the Sun-Times. Jacob and Rebecca looked at it together and exchanged several comments that were too quiet for Daniel to hear. When he was finished with the basic story he looked at David Bruce and said, "That's it in a nutshell."

"Daniel, this little project of yours is impressive," Rebecca said, "and I'd love to talk to you about it at length if we can set something up."

Before Daniel could respond David said, "Rebecca is putting together a series of articles on the power of social media and your project seems to fit right in."

Rebecca added, "And it would take the series into a totally different direction, of people creating other people. It's like this strange virtual population that no one would ever actually meet except in cyberspace."

Daniel nodded and said, "I asked my girlfriend how many of the people she encounters online can she actually verify as real people and she said only ten to twenty percent. That's pretty scary stuff."

Jacob nodded in agreement. "I read a study last week on how fewer and fewer people even use voicemail anymore. They think it takes too long. Imagine a world where we don't even talk to each other anymore."

The four of them bounced around ideas on what the article would say about the blog itself but the conversation kept coming back to Sid and his demands for payment from the Sun Times. David offered that any mention of the Sun Times situation and the way they treated Sid could make the Tribune look petty and accusatory, but then Jacob reminded everyone that they were competitors and that the Sun Times had been throwing shit at the Tribune for years. He didn't think the paper should worry about how the article might make them look. That comment prompted an idea in Daniel's head and he leaned back and said smugly, "When I get back to my desk I'm going to make a phone call, I'll fill you in tomorrow."

They talked for nearly an hour and when the meeting was over, Daniel and Rebecca had scheduled a time to meet so Daniel could work with her on an article. He and David scheduled a meeting of their own to discuss a strategy for bringing *Don't Just Stand There* to the Tribune's pages. As Daniel rode down the elevator afterward, he felt better than he had in weeks.

Wednesday September 19th

Maggie heard the incessant ringing of the doorbell all the way from the basement and she hurried up the stairs muttering,

"Geez, lighten up on the bell whoever you are." When she opened the door Jess was standing there grinning.

"Hi Maggs," he said, "I got Daniel's message to meet him here. He said it's a big deal but he didn't say what it's about."

Maggie sighed, trying to catch her breath from her run up the stairs and said, "He wouldn't tell me either, come on in." As they walked into the kitchen, she said, "He just called me from the car, he should be here any minute." She had just opened a bottle of wine and, knowing Jess loved a drink every day after work, poured him a glass without even asking him if he wanted it.

She handed it to him and said, "This has been a crazy couple of weeks around here."

Jess knew exactly what she meant. "Yeah, between the big article in the Trib and Daniel getting to start his new blog, I'll bet it's been nuts. I hope things quiet down pretty soon so he and I can get back out to the club."

"Why, so you can play golf or chase rich women?," she asked, grinning.

Jess blushed. "Come on, you make me sound like a gold digger."

"You know, if you actually tried to find a real relationship you just might find one," she said.

"Yeah, I know, Daniel tells me the same thing, but rich older women need love too." Maggie knew this was a conversation destined to go nowhere.

Jess looked out the window, saw Daniel's car pulling into the driveway and said, "Here he is." When Daniel walked in the backdoor Jess shouted, "Ooh, Daddy's home."

Daniel smiled, walked over to Maggie and kissed her. He looked over at Jess and said, "I see the kids aren't in bed yet." Maggie and Jess waited for Daniel to change his clothes and when he came back into the kitchen Maggie handed him a glass of wine. "From your message," she said, "it sounded like this is supposed to be a celebration."

Daniel was carrying a small stack of papers and laid them on the counter. "Well, actually I was thinking exactly that," he said, adding, "I'm still trying to figure out how everything happened the way it did."

"Like what?' Maggie asked.

Daniel flipped through the stack of papers he had laid on the counter and handed a copy of each page to Maggie then to Jess. "Take a minute to read this," he said, "it's a follow up to the last article in the series the Tribune did on social media. Remember, it was the one where I told them about our project with Leonard and the whole thing with Sid."

Maggie and Jess sat at the counter reading while Daniel skimmed through a copy he had made for himself. After a few minutes Maggie looked up and said, "Oh my God, did we start this?"

Jess followed with, "Holy shit, are these numbers for real?"

Daniel answered, "Maggie, the answer to your question is it sure looks like it, and Jess your answer is yes." Maggie finished reading the article, shaking her head the entire time. Jess just kept looking at Daniel without saying a word. When he saw that Maggie was finished Daniel said, "I got a call late yesterday from Rebecca Howland at the Trib. She told me the two writers who had co-written the series kept tracking a few of their sources after the last article went to print and was put up on their website.

"That was way back in July," Jess said.

"Yeah, about two months ago," Daniel replied, "and in that two month, her writers and research people saw a huge amount of internet chatter about the article and a whole lot of people were asking about the Leonard project. All kinds of people were talking about how they checked out Leonard and thought he was real. You remember, after they printed the article, how we all saw stuff coming in on Leonard's Facebook page and on Linked In, from people who didn't want to believe that he wasn't real. Little by little the whole thing spread and people have started making up their own Leonard Paduszkas. Rebecca said her writers have tracked nearly a thousand of their readers who have said they have already done it or plan to do it."

"Shit," Jess said, "and we gave them the damned instruction manual."

Maggie, true to her background in the world of lawyers and litigation, asked, "Can what we did be construed in any way as against the law?"

"Nope," Daniel answered, "I made it a point to cover that with Rebecca. She was already talking with the newspaper's legal counsel and they said all the article did was report the facts and did not endorse or encourage what we did."

Jess interrupted, "We can't be the first ones to create a fake identity like we did with Leonard, I'm sure its been done before"

Daniel shook his head and replied, "No we probably weren't the first, but like you said, we wrote the instruction manual and let it get out to one of the largest media companies in the country."

"And just think," Maggie said, "we did this whole thing in our spare time. Just think what a person or a group could do if they devoted all their time to it."

"Yeah," Jess added, "all those high school nerds and slackers could create more fake people than you could ever count."

"Forget the slackers," Daniel countered, "just think of what a large, well-funded company or political group could pull off."

Maggie looked at Daniel. "I can see why you said you didn't know how to feel about all this, it's pretty scary stuff."

Daniel asked her, "Maggs, do you remember when we started this little project and I asked you how many of the people you encounter online you knew personally, and you said ten to twenty percent?" Maggie nodded. "And you said you assumed the other eighty to ninety percent of the people were legitimate." Maggie didn't say a word. "Well honey, it looks like we're heading for a world where you won't be able to take that much on faith anymore. It's gonna be a world where everyone you encounter online could be as real as Leonard Paduszka. It will be like there's a whole other world of fake people doing fake things and interacting with the real ones, and you'll never realize the difference."

Jess chimed in, "So what's the other stuff? You said everything that has happened."

Well, after my first meeting with the Sun Times I got the idea that there might be a way for Sid to come out of this thing with some kind of a win, so I called Doug Stewart again."

"What, and asked him again to pay Sid the money?" Jess asked.

"Nope," Daniel answered, "something even better. I told Stewart about the Tribune series and how our little project with Leonard would be a part of it. I made it clear that the article would tell the whole story, including the Sun Times' refusal to compensate Sid for his photograph." Maggie and Jess were smiling as Daniel continued. "I didn't threaten the guy or cop any kind of attitude. I merely suggested that a happy ending to Sid's story, maybe like a job on the Sun Times' loading dock or housekeeping staff would make for a warm and fuzzy feeling for everyone involved in this thing."

"And how did Stewart react to the idea?" Maggie asked.

"I was surprised," Daniel answered, "He said he'd go along with it and he didn't even have to clear it with his fucking lawyers. I think he knew the potential harm the article could do to the paper's reputation, so in a way it was a Hobson's choice for him. And it's kind of ironic that giving a job to a poor homeless man makes them look good even though they originally intended to fuck him over. Stewart told me he'd set things in motion."

The three of them raised a toast to the rebirth of the blog and to the good news about Sid. They talked some more and Jess said that he had to head home so he could call his new romantic partner in private. He stopped as he opened the door, turned to Daniel and Maggie and said, "I think we all know what we have to do now, but how about if we meet here again, tomorrow at seven-ish? I'll have a little surprise for you."

Daniel looked at Maggie, who had the same quizzical look on her face. "Okay," he said somewhat reluctantly.

Thursday September 20th

Daniel and Maggie got home within a few minutes of each other and quickly changed their clothes. Jess' plan to meet them at seven put a crimp in their normal dinner schedule so Maggie put together a small plate of cheeses and olives while Daniel opened a bottle of Chardonnay. At seven-fifteen they saw the headlights of Jess' car as he pulled into the driveway, and a minute later, heard his knock, immediately followed by the opening of the door. He took one step inside and called out, "Ladies and gentlemen, it's my honor to introduce you to the new Materials Handling Assistant for the Chicago Tribune, Mr. Sidney Kubek!" Jess stepped to his left as Daniel and Maggie saw the slender, tanned and smiling man behind him.

Daniel grinned and said, "Hey Sid, come on in, it's so great to finally meet you." Sid entered slowly, looking nervous and shy.

Maggie extended her hand and said, "Welcome Sid, would you like a glass of wine?"

Sid's smile never faded and he answered, "Yes . . . please, I mean . . . thank you."

Daniel looked over at Jess. "You were right when you said you had a surprise."

Jess grinned and said, "Well, last night I think we all knew what needed to be done and I thought it was only fair for Sid to be a part of it."

"And I couldn't agree more," Maggie replied.

Daniel said, "I'll be right back, Sid, Jess, make yourselves at home." He walked into the spare bedroom that he and Maggie used as a home office and came back into the kitchen carrying a paper shredder and a small metal wastebasket. He placed them on the counter and plugged in the shredder.

Sid had a confused look on his face and Jess said, "Sid, the little project that we needed your picture for, well it's all over and tonight we're going to officially shut it down."

Sid nodded and seemed to understand as Daniel moved to stand in front of the shredder and announce, "Okay," he said," the good news is that maybe all of this will make people so unsure of who is and isn't real that they'll pick up their phones to call people again, or even knock on their door for some face time."

"And is there bad news?" Jess asked.

Daniel picked up the tattered yellow file folder from the counter. "Well, I think it's time we said our farewells to Leonard Allen Paduszka. Let's all go online tonight and shut everything down. Remove every trace that Leonard ever existed."

Both Jess and Maggie nodded but Sid's look of confusion had returned. Jess looked at Sid and said, "He means all of the stuff on the computer, Sid."

Daniel turned on the shredder and the three of them took turns feeding the contents of the file into the jaws of the machine while Sid sipped his wine and watched. Daniel couldn't help but think that it all felt like a funeral. When every page was gone and the birth certificate and Social Security card were also destroyed, Daniel held the one remaining item in his left hand. It was an 8 by 10 color photograph of Sid, a.k.a. Leonard, and Daniel said, "Sid, why don't you take care of this one?" He handed the photo to Sid, and the slender, quiet man slowly slipped it into the shredde'rs feed slot." His look of confusion seemed to have changed to one of sad recognition.

For a few moments there was silence, and then Daniel said, "Everyone, please pick up your wine glasses and raise a toast to our friend Leonard, a good man who died too young." Then he turned toward Sid and said, "and also to our new friend Sid, a good man who has been reborn."

"The Bandit & THE Barista"

1

Even though I was fifteen minutes ahead of my usual drive time to the office, I wasn't able to beat the crowd and long line at Starbucks. I was number seven in line with five more visibly impatient coffee drinkers behind me. I scanned the faces of my fellow patrons, mostly people in business attire waiting for the caffeine fix that would help them navigate the commute to their various places of employment.

Through my morning visits I had come to recognize many of the regular customers and I even knew their regular coffee orders. There was the pretty young redhead with the fake fingernails who ordered a Grande Caramel Macchiato with extra whipped cream, and the heavy-set bald man who loved his daily Venti Americano with an extra shot. This morning I paid particular attention to the man just ahead of me in line. I knew from the way the baristas called out the man's name when his order was ready that his first name was John so I had named him John Doe. John bore a remarkable resemblance to me; about the same height and weight, the same dark brown hair but John Doe slicked his back. We even had strong facial similarities. An odd thing about John Doe was that he always wore black clothes and large, wrap-around, tortoise-shell framed sunglasses, every day, rain or shine. Even inside Starbucks he never took off those shades. I always wondered why people wore shades indoors. Did they think it made them look cool, like a movie star or hip-hop singer? Whenever I was at the casino I saw a lot of that, mostly men in expensive looking clothes and designer shades, trying to look like high rollers.

John Doe's drink of choice was a Tall Latte with cinnamon and vanilla. To me it seemed like something a young girl would order, but then, Starbucks made a fortune catering to people's whims and self-indulgences. But Brad Chase is a more basic type. My standing order is a Grande black coffee, nothing fancy or pretentious, just good, strong unadulterated java. I finally reached the counter and placed my order with Becky, a round faced and very talkative young barista who seemed to be on the job every day. Today she had her long, dark hair pulled tightly back into a bun, making her face look even larger. "Hi Brad," she said cheerfully, "How are you today?" "I'm fine, Becky, how are you?" "Oh, okay I guess except my cat's sick and I'm so worried about her. She won't eat or drink and I can't afford a big bill from the vet and I don't know what to do. She's only four years old and she's almost never sick so I tried changing her food but that didn't work so I don't know what to do next." I listened patiently, secretly feeling sorry for a cat that had to endure that kind of constant chatter. Finally she took a breath brushed away a wisp of blonde hair from her eyes and asked, "Want the regular again today?" I nodded and she continued her cat story while she poured my coffee. I handed her three dollars, told her to keep the change and added, "Good luck with the cat." I quickly headed for the door to get out of earshot before she started talking again, but I could still hear her telling her cat story again to the woman who had been behind me in line. John Doe had just picked up his latte from the counter and we reached the door at the same time. I smiled and held open the door. John Doe nodded, said "Thanks," and walked toward the parking lot. I saw him get into a silver-gray Toyota sedan that looked a lot like my wife's silver-gray Nissan. As generic and ordinary looking as two cars could be.

I found it hard to keep my mind on the traffic and my driving as I headed toward his office. I couldn't stop thinking about my gambling and how it was impacting my bank account and my personal life. I needed a change of fortune. During the past weekend my visit to the Lone Mountain Indian casino just extended my string of bad luck. I avoided the slot machines because there was no way to engage them or use any kind of strategy. I always preferred blackjack and dice games, games where I could study the other players, follow the action and decide when and what to bet. Yet every time I thought I had the odds figured out and made my move everything just seemed to blow up in my face. Somehow, sooner or later, the odds would turn in my favor if I just kept trying.

As I made the slow descent down the ramp into my office parking garage I set my Starbucks cup back into the cup holder and pulled my access card from the clip on the sun visor. The mechanics of my daily routine had become mind-numbingly boring. I knew that all I needed was a big score at the tables to get enough money to change things, to have a chance to be free of the monotony my life had become. I drove through the security gate and pulled into my parking space, gathered up my laptop bag and coffee cup and headed for the elevator.

I stood there with four silent strangers pretending to be fascinated as the overhead panel display showed the downward path of the elevator. A voice behind me said, "Mornin' Mr. Chase." I turned and saw the young man who had just started working as an intern in the office the previous week. "Hey, Tyler, how are you?" I asked half-heartedly. The tall, gangly twenty-something answered, "Oh, fine I guess, for a Monday." We stood there waiting for the doors to open. I sipped my now tepid coffee, not really interested in making conversation, but the eager Tyler was obviously in the mood to talk. "Hey man, did you watch the ASU game Saturday? That comeback was amazing." I took a gulp of coffee and said, "Nah, I was at the casino most of the day." The elevator doors opened and I waited for Tyler to step through. As we rode to the seventh floor Justin continued his enthusiastic retelling of the details of Saturday's football game. I tried to feign interest and was glad that there were no stops on the way. When the doors opened I quickly swung to the left toward my office and called back over my shoulder, "See ya, Tyler."

After a brief stop in the employee lunchroom to reheat my coffee in the microwave I headed down the corridor to my office. The dark, empty offices I passed along the way were a daily reminder of how badly the company had fared during the recession. At its peak, Chandler Construction had been a strong and very busy company with 145 employees in the headquarters office. Now, after four years of a major building slump and corporate right-sizing it was down to a mere 34 people. The company was less than a month away from moving into a smaller office space on the third floor, and even though there had been a slight upturn in the number of new projects, my role as the head of marketing was under the microscope. I knew I had to bring in a substantial project very soon or I too might become a casualty.

By 10:15 AM I had returned my e-mails and a few voice messages. I sat at my computer, went online to get my personal bank statement, and then just stared at the screen. For years I had maintained a modest but comfortable five-figure savings account for myself, separate from my wife Jenna's savings or our shared accounts. Jenna had received a substantial trust fund three years earlier when her father died and she had willingly put it into an account that I had access to as well. My lust for gambling had slowly and steadily eroded most of my own savings, and when I managed one night to lose two thousand dollars from Jenna's trust fund account, she found out and confronted me. She told me she thought I had a gambling addiction but I argued that the casino was just a way to relieve the stress from my job. She reminded me that I had promised to never touch the trust fund money without talking with her first, and I responded with a lame comment that I was doing it for both of us, not just myself.

I had never been good at arguing with her. All in all we got along great. Jenna's demeanor and easy going ways seemed to fit her quiet beauty. She still looked like the pretty, little blonde I met in college, and looking into her big, hazel eyes still softened whatever anger I might have felt. Our disagreements never seemed to last very long. So when several weeks had gone by without more tension or arguing I really thought that things had calmed down.

When I got home Saturday night and Jenna found out I had lost more money that day, the tone of our conversation was something totally new. We argued more loudly and angrily than ever before. I stormed out of the house, went to a nearby sports bar and when I got back home around 2:00 AM Jenna was asleep, or pretending to be. Given the circumstances I wasn't surprised when, on Sunday morning, she told me she was going to fly back to Virginia to see her mother for a week or so. I totally understood. She made me agree to sign documents that barred me from accessing her trust fund. I felt humiliated but I agreed and when I got home from work on Monday Jenna laid the paperwork out on the kitchen counter and watched as I signed it. I knew she was furious and I also knew our marriage was on shaky ground. For the rest of the evening she barely spoke to me and we didn't make direct eye contact once. When I drove her to the airport on Monday morning she kept herself turned away from me, staring out her side window without speaking, and when I stopped at the terminal I pulled her two bags from the trunk and set them on the sidewalk in front of her. I leaned toward her, hoping to kiss her, and said, "Have a good flight honey." She gave me a quick, expressionless glance, pulled up the handles on her wheelie-bags, turned and walked through the double doors without responding.

My drive to the office seemed to take twice as long as usual. My marriage problems, the pressure at work and my need to get back the money I'd lost all worked on my mind, and by noon

I'd had enough. I told my assistant that I wasn't feeling well and was going to go home to lie down. I wasn't really hungry but I stopped at a small restaurant for a sandwich and a beer. Two hours and four beers later I left for home.

2

The evening news was on the television but it was only background noise as I lay on the sofa staring at the ceiling. After hours of thinking and worrying about my problems I could only come up with two courses of action. I could try to go cold turkey and quit gambling totally, and accept my losses without making them any worse, or I could come up with a way to get some quick cash, take it to the casino and try to win enough to give back to Jenna what I'd taken from her account. The thought of losing her was the worst part of the situation and that fact steered me toward a decision. If I stopped gambling now I knew there would be no way I could get back all of my losses. I would make one last try, concentrate on the blackjack tables where my luck didn't seem so bad, and win enough to at least cover the money I'd taken from Jenna. It seemed like the only thing to do.

I got up from the sofa and went into the bedroom to change into a sweat suit, then microwaved a leftover chicken breast and a small container of carrots and sat back down in front of the television to eat. How many evenings during my bachelor days had I done the same thing at dinnertime? It was lonely then and felt even lonelier now. I thought of calling Jenna but I knew she wouldn't be ready to talk to me yet so I picked up my cellphone and texted her a brief message, "*I miss you and I'm sorry. Don't give up on me.*" I finished eating and put the dishes into the dishwasher, then flopped back down on the sofa. I kept waiting for the chime on my phone to signal a text message but, not surprisingly, it never came. Finally I went to bed and laid there thinking about my situation. I had decided on what I wanted to do to solve my problem but had no clue how I was going to get the cash, and I eventually fell asleep without one.

The Tuesday morning crowd at Starbucks seemed bigger than usual and I had to park next door in front of the bank. It was only about a hundred feet from Starbucks entrance but the distance was still a major nuisance to me on a morning when I was feeling anything but patient. As I was getting out of my car I saw John Doe walking out of Starbucks toward his silver gray Toyota. I watched the man in the black clothes and wrap-around, tortoise shell framed sunglasses and slicked-back hair artfully juggle his Tall Latte with cinnamon and vanilla while getting into his car, and an idea came to me like divine intervention. The bank had cash on hand and I needed some. If I could enter and leave the bank quickly, the teller and any witnesses would have a description of the man who robbed the bank. A tall, slender man with slicked-back brown hair dressed in black and wrap-around tortoise shell framed shades. He was carrying a Starbucks cup in the bank and when he left he drove away in a small silver-gray sedan.

I waited and watched John Doe drive away. My idea for robbing the bank seemed too simple but that meant it would be easier to pull off. It would be quick and clean, in and out in a minute or two, with a culprit who would be very easy to describe to the police. But my conscience stopped my scheming right then and there. I would be framing an innocent man for the crime, a man I didn't know, a man who might have a family to support and who didn't deserve to have his life torn apart. I liked the part of my plan that pointed the finger of blame toward someone else but I had to figure out a way to make sure that man wouldn't actually be convicted of the robbery. I'd have to set things in motion in such a way that, eventually I could get John Doe off the hook. And the entire scheme had to happen before Jenna got back home.

I sent Jenna three more text messages while I was at work but got no replies. Finally, while I was sitting at the kitchen table eating my carry-out pizza dinner my phoned chimed with a message. It was from Jenna, and all it said was, *"Having a nice visit with Mom, it's really cold here."* It wasn't exactly a warm, romantic kind of message but I felt buoyed by the fact that she had at least communicated. With the three hour time difference between us, I typed a simple reply, *"Good night honey, stay warm."* I finished my pizza, cleaned up the kitchen and went into the living room, and after making sure all the window blinds were closed I pulled a yellow legal pad and pen from my computer bag then sat down on the sofa. Between clicking from TV channel to TV channel, sipping a glass of last night's leftover wine and glancing around at the closed blinds, I wrote down the framework for my plan to rob the bank.

The strong physical resemblance between John Doe and me was the key to pulling off the plan but I knew I needed more than that, some other small details that could be used as evidence by the police. And every one of those little details could also be used by me to help set the man free if I figured everything carefully. I drew a line down the middle of a legal pad. On the left I wrote the heading *"EVIDENCE IN"* and on the right side of the line I wrote *"EVIDENCE OUT"*. I figured that every separate thing that the police would use to charge John Doe with the robbery had to have a back door that I could use later to create doubt as to who it was that really robbed the bank.

First and foremost, the bank's security cameras would record John Doe entering the bank and would track him every second he was inside as well as follow him as he went outside to his car. I would have to make sure his appearance matched every detail of John Doe's signature look. I had a black shirt and slacks and I knew I could buy some kind of hair gel to slick back my hair. I would go to Sunglass Hut in the mall and find a pair of big, wrap-around, tortoise shell shades. I was confident that, if I did everything right, I could be a dead ringer for the unsuspecting man. The camera images alone could probably convict a person of a crime and I couldn't undo that part of the evidence. It would have to be something else, something the police would use as they built their case, that I could use later to show that John Doe didn't really commit the crime.

The bottle of wine was half gone and my legal pad still had only the two headings. I was struggling to find ideas I could use and then it hit me. Starbucks! The regular customers each had a first name and a regular drink selection. It was their identity. It's what Becky the barista remembered about each person who stepped up to the counter and she even wrote the customer's first name on the cup. I could use this in building my scheme. When I walked up to the bank teller dressed as John Doe I'd also be holding John Doe's drink of choice, a Tall Latte with cinnamon and vanilla, and I'd leave the half-empty cup sitting on the teller counter. It would be a link to the Starbucks next door and to John Doe. I felt like my plan was starting to gel but I still needed more detail. When I approached the teller window I couldn't speak because the teller would hear my voice and it might not sound like John Doe's voice. I'd have to slip the teller a note asking for the money. Then another idea struck me. I would write the note in red pen on a yellow legal pad and tear the note portion of the sheet off the pad, leaving a torn, partial sheet hanging behind. I'd wait for John Doe to park at Starbucks and when he went through the front door I would open his car door and slip the legal pad under the driver's seat in a way that it wouldn't be seen.

Under *"EVIDENCE IN"* I had written "Starbucks Cup" and "Yellow Legal Pad for Note". The space under *"EVIDENCE OUT"* was still blank. For every piece of evidence that pointed toward John Doe I had to come up with another one that would point the other way. I was far from being an expert on criminal investigations but I had watched enough cop movies and television shows to have an idea of what happened at a crime scene. I also figured that whatever the police found would stay a secret until the case went to trial. Sometime before that happened I knew I would have to contact the police with my inside information and get John Doe out of his jam. After a few more minutes of staring at the pad I had my answers. Under "*EVIDENCE OUT*" next to "Starbucks Cup" I wrote "Tall Latte with Cinnamon and Vanilla." The police would no doubt check the contents of the cup, and if I notified them with the fact I knew what the drink was, they would wonder how an outsider would know that fact. Under "*EVIDENCE OUT*" next to "Yellow Legal Pad for Note" I wrote "Hide Message in Pad." The note to the teller would be written in red ink and left at the scene. I would write a message to the police somewhere further back in the legal pad in the same red ink, and only I would know what it said until I contacted the investigators. As I thought through my plan I decided that contacting the cops through regular mail would be the safest way because they couldn't trace it back to me. "Good old snail mail," I thought, "it's still good for something."

I looked at my notes again, then under "*EVIDENCE IN*" I wrote, "Silver Gray Toyota Sedan", and under "*EVIDENCE OUT*" I wrote "Silver Gray Nissan Sedan." As long as I could exit the bank parking lot in a way that no one could get a clear look at my license plate, I figured the strong similarities between the two generic looking cars would be an important link. That was the biggest reason I had to make this all happen before Jenna got home.

3

I managed to put in a full day at the office and still get a few errands finished. Chandler Construction had been awarded a thirty-five million dollar warehouse and fulfillment center project and that took a lot of pressure off of my shoulders and bought me some time. I had two other potential clients that I was courting and the work side of my troubles seemed to be improving. I still had to deal with replacing the money in Jenna's trust fund and figure out a way to fix my marital issues, and that was enough stress for anyone to deal with. The little thing about robbing a bank added to the mix only made things seem more daunting. Jenna and I had exchanged two text messages during the course of the day and I was tempted to call her on the phone, but I figured it was best to let her decide when the time was right to talk. I thought about Jenna during my entire drive home that evening.

I stood hunched over at the kitchen counter with all of the elements of my scheme laid out in front of me. There was a small bottle of Garnier Fructis Ultra-strong Sleek & Shine hair gel, a pair of Oakley Stingray wraparound tortoise shell frame sunglasses, brand new yellow legal pads, a red felt-tip pen and even a half-empty Starbucks cup. I had stopped at a different Starbucks location on my way home to order the Tall Latte with cinnamon and vanilla and when the barista asked me for my name I said, "John." I watched her write it on the side of the cup. I made sure that I held the cup only by the brown cardboard sleeve. My long sleeve black shirt and black slacks were hanging in the bedroom and I had checked the gas gauge in Jenna's car just to make sure there was enough gas for the short round trip between our house and the bank. I unzipped a blue oversized security deposit bag that I had purchased at an office supply store on my lunch hour. It was the kind of sturdy, nylon bag that small business owners used when they made cash deposits. Carrying it into the bank would look like a totally normal, day-to-day occurrence.

I scanned the array of items spread out in front of me then went out to the garage. I pulled out a pair of disposable latex gloves from a twelve-pair package that I had bought to use on a painting project in the living room. I had to make sure that my fingerprints didn't show up on the legal pad or coffee cup, otherwise my entire plan would blow up in my face. When I got back to the kitchen counter I put on the gloves and slipped the cardboard sleeve from the cup, tore it open, then wrapped it back around the cup. That would make it easier for me to take the sleeve with me when I left the cup behind at the bank. I peeled the cellophane wrapper off the three-pack of legal pads and laid one in front of me on the counter, then picked up the red pen. I thought for a moment then slowly lettered my robbery note to the teller, *"DON'T SAY OR DO ANYTHING UNUSUAL. THIS IS A ROBBERY. EMPTY ALL YOUR BILLS INTO THE BAG. DO IT FAST AND DO IT NOW."*

The message sounded right to me, not that I knew anything about robbing banks or what to say to a teller in that kind of situation. It was short, to the point and I hoped just menacing enough to motivate the teller to comply. Now I had to write the message that would get John Doe off the hook. I tore the portion of the paper that contained the note from the rest of the first page then counted back fifteen pages and started to write at the top of that page, *"YOU HAVE THE WRONG GUY, I ROBBED YOUR DAMN BANK"*. Under that I drew a smiley face. I closed up the pad, looked again at the pieces of my first venture into the world of a criminal, and slowly walked into the bedroom. I was more than a little nervous and I lay in bed most of the night wondering if I could and should do what I had planned. I was just an ordinary, average guy and I had never even imagined myself committing a crime. I started to wonder if I had moved too quickly in deciding on a way out of my dilemma. If I got caught it would be the end of everything, my marriage, my career and even my social life. But my plan seemed solid and if I pulled it off as cleanly as I thought it could go, I could get back the money I took from Jenna and then some. After that I would try hard, really hard, to curb my activity at the casino. I felt confident that I could do it all in a way that would also get John Doe off the hook. Despite my confidence it was a very long night.

4

I sat in the car watching the activity in front of the bank and in Starbucks. Knowing this would not be a typical weekday morning I had sent my assistant an e-mail saying I'd be into the office a little bit late. It was 8:25 AM and the regular customers that I usually ran into in line were already showing up. The bank didn't open until 9:00 AM. At 8:35 a silver gray Toyota pulled into a parking space about a hundred feet from Starbuck's sidewalk and a moment later John Doe got out and walked inside to get his order. I scanned the parking lot then drove over and stopped Jenna's car behind the Toyota. I pulled on my latex gloves and took the yellow legal pad from the seat beside me, then walked over to the Toyota and opened the passenger door. I quickly slipped the pad under the driver's seat and made sure that it wouldn't be visible when someone entered from either side of the car. Then I shut the door, got back into Jenna's Nissan and drove back to my vantage point near the bank. I had a clear view of the steady stream of people entering and exiting Starbucks. About five minutes later John Doe came out and headed for his car. I stared at him then looked at myself in the rearview mirror. The hair gel and wraparound shades had transformed me into a very passable version of the other man. I watched John Doe drive away and wondered how long it would be before the Phoenix police were at the man's door.

I moved my car and backed into a parking space along the side of the bank where there were no windows. My license plate wouldn't be visible from passersby and I could pull straight out into traffic to make my getaway. At 9:01 AM I picked up the Starbucks cup from the cup holder, made sure my note to the teller was neatly tucked into my shirt pocket, held my blue deposit bag and opened the car door. A sudden wave of panic engulfed me and I steadied myself on the car door and took several slow, deep breaths. It wasn't too late to back out and go with Plan B, but Plan B seemed like a sure way to a ruined life and Plan A, the robbery plan, had at least a shot at success. I stood by the car for a moment, collecting myself and checking out the area around the bank entrance. There was just one other customer walking into the bank and a woman standing at the ATM to the left of the entrance doors. I figured that was about as empty as I could ever expect the bank to be. I walked quickly and directly toward the door and as I entered I made a quick scan of the business lobby. Everything around me seemed to be moving at half speed and my mind seemed to tune out every sound. I picked a teller, a short, heavy-set young woman who looked like she hadn't been in the working world very long. "Good," I thought as I approached her, "she looks like a rookie."

As I got to the teller window the young woman smiled and said, "Good morning sir, how are you this morning?" I quietly muttered "Fine." I set my Starbucks cup on the edge of the counter and slipped off the cardboard sleeve, my hand never touching the cup itself. I slipped the sleeve into the pocket of my slacks. With my other hand I reached for my shirt pocket and, carefully gripping the note between my knuckles, I pulled it out and laid it on the counter in front of her. The woman unfolded it and Id watched as her smile disappeared. For a moment she stood there frozen, and when I gently knocked my clenched fist on the counter she put her hand to her mouth then opened the cash drawer. I smiled at her, trying to appear as normal and unassuming as possible and slid the unzipped deposit bag toward her. The words in my note must have been compelling enough because she quickly emptied the cash drawer into the bag. My eyes scanned the array of security cameras on the wall behind the teller and I knew that one or more of them were looking right at me. I turned for a moment and saw more cameras on each side of the entrance. When the frightened young woman was finished filling the bag I took tit from her, turned and zipped it closed as I walked toward the front door. I fought the urge to look back or make eye contact with anyone. Between the sounds of my heels on the terrazzo floor I listened for voices or any kind of sound that indicated the teller had alerted anyone or tripped an alarm. I heard nothing out of the ordinary and stepped up my pace.

When I got outside and around the corner of the building I started to run to my car. With keys in hand, I started it and a few seconds later I was driving through the parking lot. The dashboard clock read 9:06 AM. In about thirty more seconds I reached the traffic light at the shopping center entrance, made a quick right turn into traffic and headed for home.

My heart was pounding and I had to grip the steering wheel tightly to keep my hands from shaking. My first task was to get home and get the silver gray car into the garage and out of sight. Our house was normally a three or four minute drive from Starbucks but I was driving much faster than usual. "Careful man," I thought to myself, "don't speed, the last thing you need is to catch the attention of a passing cop." At 9:12 AM I pressed the pad of the garage door opener on the visor and drove into the garage and lowered the door the moment the car came to a stop. I sat there for a moment, breathing hard and trying to regain my composure. I kept looking in the rearview mirror as if someone was behind him. Finally, I took the blue deposit bag from the seat beside me, got out of the car and stuffed it into a storage cabinet behind some old paint cans and tools, then did the same with the wraparound sunglasses. I walked into the house and started taking off the black shirt as I headed down the hallway to the bedroom. A quick shower and shampoo got rid of the thick hair gel and in minutes John Doe was gone and Brad Chase was back.

By the time I got to his office it was already 11:00 AM and there was a half-written marketing report that I had to finish, a long chain of e-mails waiting for my attention and a lunch meeting with a client I'd been courting for over a year. On a normal day it would have been a struggle to stay focused and get things done, but when I added to the equation the fact I had just committed a major felony to offset my gambling losses, my ability to concentrate was all but gone. By mid-afternoon I figured that something about the robbery might have made it to the local news media, but a quick on-line search on my laptop turned up nothing. I was usually a laid-back, take life as it comes kind of guy but I had reached a point where the robbery was the only thing on my mind. Trying to work or talk or think about anything else was pointless. Even the warm, affectionate and hopeful sounding text message I'd received from Jenna was a distant second in my mind.

I managed to get through the rest of the workday and stopped for an early dinner at a Chili's restaurant near the house. I sat at the bar and asked the bartender to turn the usual sports channel to one with the local news. After sitting through two stories about local politics and what seemed like a dozen commercials, the story of the bank robbery came on the air. I stared at the screen and listened intently, but was surprised at how little the reporter said, just that a Phoenix branch of Bank of America had been robbed that morning, the robber walked off with an undisclosed amount of cash and that Phoenix police and bank officials were continuing their investigation.

I leaned back in my stool, took a long sip of my beer as another commercial came on. "Shit,", I thought, "is that all there is? They must have found something, the coffee cup or the note or something." Strangely, I was almost deflated. I'd robbed a damn bank, put my whole life on the line and the story got about forty-five seconds of airtime. But after a few more sips of beer and a lot more thinking about it I realized that the police had to move carefully and methodically, build their case to not only find the thief but to also make the charges stand up in court. "Just sit tight, man" I told myself, "they'll pick up on the clues in time, just be patient." I finished my sandwich and my second beer and headed for home.

5

After I changed my clothes I tried to look through the day's mail but I knew that blue nylon zipper bag in the garage, with the undisclosed amount of cash inside, was my first priority. I walked into the garage and pulled the bag from behind the paint cans and carried it back into the kitchen. Just holding and looking at it in made me nervous and my hands started to shake just like they did when I was at the bank. Despite having all day to calm down, the whole situation still seemed surreal to me. I was standing at my kitchen counter holding a bag full of stolen cash and I was the guy that had stolen it. How did I get to this point in just a few days?

I looked down at the bag and muttered, "Okay, let's see what my little caper produced." I unzipped it and poured the contents on to the counter. "My god," I thought as I looked at the pile of bills, "this is like something from a freaking movie." I went to the window and closed the blinds, looked around the room as if to make sure no one was watching then went back to the counter. My hands ruffled aimlessly through the pile, like I was trying to count the cash by sense of touch. The teller had grabbed the money separately by denomination, so the pile started with singles at one end and progressed to fifties and hundreds at the other. I carefully sorted through each denomination and put them into neat and separate stacks. Before the robbery I had no idea what to expect the amount would be. I figured there was probably a thousand dollars or so in a typical teller's drawer, but that was not based on any kind of inside knowledge or facts. It was just another item to add to my long list of things I didn't know about robbing a bank.

The counting process was slow and I wrote down each subtotal on a small notepad I'd pulled from the utility drawer in front of me. The more I sorted and counted the more my heart raced. When I finished my tally and wrote down the total I just stared at the pad; three thousand, four hundred and fifty dollars. I checked my math twice and each time the result was the same. Once again I scanned the room and looked at the closed window blinds, and then walked over to make sure the door from the garage was locked. "Holy shit," I said aloud. The amount was way more than the two-thousand dollars I needed to put back in Jenna's trust fund. I could just make up a story that I had won big at blackjack while she was gone and made enough to pay back her account. I figured that might be enough to calm her down and put the whole thing behind us, and still leave me with a big wad of cash to take to the tables.

On Saturday I could get to the casino early, before the weekend evening crowds clogged the blackjack tables. The pile of cash in front of me suddenly seemed intoxicating. I ran my hands lightly over each stack, already thinking about how I could move up from the twenty-five dollar tables to the one-hundred dollar ones. My daydream of being a big time player was interrupted by a text from Jenna that said, "Its late, going to bed now. I'll call you in AM, love you." I read the message a second time and smiled. In the morning I'd be talking to my wife for the first time in a week, and the signs seemed to indicate she was in a much more forgiving frame of mind.

At 10:00 PM I turned on the local news and after about ten minutes the reporter began the story about the robbery. This report was a bit more detailed than the earlier one. It mentioned that the security cameras recorded the robber's image, that he was seen leaving the scene in a silver gray car and that the police had other evidence they were pursuing. "Great," I thought. "maybe the stuff I planted will actually work." I had walked through the whole thing in my mind a dozen times during the day and thought I had a loose idea of what the police would do. If they were smart they'd look beyond the fact the Starbucks cup I left on the teller counter had the name John written on it. The latte with vanilla and cinnamon was a very pungent drink and, I guessed, would be easy for someone to identify. That, along with the security video, would lead them to John Doe and that would lead them to his silver gray car with the yellow legal pad under the seat. I wondered how long it would take them to get that far in their investigation.

I was already up, showered and dressed when Jenna called the next morning. I saw her name on the screen of my phone and felt as nervous as I was excited. I took a slow breath, pressed the connect icon and said, "Mornin' honey." There was a pause then Jenna said, "Mornin' yourself, how are you?" I dropped on to a stool at the kitchen counter. "Oh, fine I guess, but this bachelor lifestyle is really wearing thin." I heard Jenna laugh softly and she asked, "Are you eating anything besides bar food?" "Oh hell yes," I answered, "pizza, leftovers and an occasional bowl of cereal, all the things you'd expect." There was another pause and I asked, "How is your mom, doing okay?" "Yeah, she's fine but she seems so much older and more frail than when I visited last year." "Well, I guess that's to be expected when you're seventy-five. Age happens."

The longer they talked the better I felt, and nearly twenty minutes later Jenna said, "Hey I have to run, I promised Mom I'd take her to lunch then do some shopping." Another pause and then she asked, "What are you going to do this weekend?" I could hear something in her voice. "Oh, nothing special, probably watch the college games all day and the NFL games on Sunday. Jay called me yesterday about maybe golfing in the morning so I guess I have a few options." I was half expecting her to say something like, "Please don't gamble," but she just sighed and said, "Well, just relax and enjoy yourself. You have my itinerary for my trip home on Tuesday, right?" "Yep, its right here on the side of the fridge. I'll see you at the north side arrival area at 1:30." "Sounds good," she said. I waited a few seconds then said, "I love you Jenna." Another pause, then she said, "I know, I love you too."

I had left my friend Jay's golf invitation up in the air so I called him to say that I had to take care of a few things that couldn't wait so maybe they could try for next week. The few things I had to take care of were on the craps and blackjack tables. I thought again about the tone of Jenna's voice. Mys gambling had become a huge issue in our marriage but somehow I believed I had reached a turning point. I had stuck two the thousand dollars for Jenna's account into a manila envelope and slipped it under the mattress. Two hundred dollars went into my wallet and the rest of the cash was in a smaller envelope that would fit into the inside pocket of my sport coat. It was my ticket to solving my problems once and for all.

6

I walked through the casino's front doors at 2:00 PM. It was busier than I had expected but still nothing near the crowds that would start showing up in a few hours. It had always been easier to get a place at the twenty-five dollar blackjack tables in the afternoon. When I walked past them and got to the array of hundred-dollar tables there were only four people playing. "Great," I thought, "no distractions, no noise and no bullshit, just me and the cards." But another part of me wished I was playing the tables in the evening. I'd be standing there, Brad Chase, with all of the big hitters, the guys in sunglasses and expensive suits with huge piles of chips stacked in front of them. "Maybe someday," I thought to himself.

By 3:15 PM I was down four hundred dollars. I had won a few hands but lost a lot more and I couldn't seem to find my groove. I considered himself to be a decent blackjack player despite my overall losing record. I compared it to my golf game, where I'd shoot in the high nineties a dozen times but then a round of eighty-four made me believe I was actually a pretty good golfer. But the truth was I was really the high nineties kind of player. After losing another hundred I decided to find out if the dice would be kinder to me than the cards and walked down the concourse to the craps tables.

I looked at my watch at 4:10 PM. In less than an hour I had lost another three hundred dollars playing craps. The higher-stakes tables weren't as exciting as I had imagined they would be. And I was faced with the cold, hard fact that my gambling skills were exactly the same as they'd always been, I was just losing money in bigger chunks. I was down seven hundred dollars, had a few hundred left and had no reason to believe my luck would change. I decided to walk back to the blackjack tables for one last try.

I stood at a different table than the one I'd already lost on and spent about ten minutes watching the play. Two men were playing from opposite sides of the table. Player One was a heavy-set, middle-aged man who seemed to be sweating profusely, and the lack of chips in front of him meant he wasn't exactly on a winning streak. Player Two was younger, better dressed and had a constant smile as he placed his bets and called the cards. The three stacks of chips at his spot seemed to be his reason for smiling. I enjoyed watching other people play the game because there were so many strategies and so many so-called guaranteed methods for counting cards, even though the House did everything possible to watch for it and stop it. Counting cards was, I had heard, the best way to be a steady winner as long as you could keep anyone from detecting it.

The dealer, a very attractive young brunette, deftly pulled the cards from the shoe and flipped them to the two men, then took her own two cards. Her up card was a ten. Player One appeared to be very nervous and hesitated, while Player Two, showing a nine and an Ace, immediately said, "Stay." Player One, showing a five and a nine, sighed, tapped the table and said, "Hit me." The dealer laid a card in front of him, he flipped it and the dealer said, "And it's a King, sorry sir it's not your day." Then she flipped her down card and said, "Dealer shows a five." Player Two said "I'll stay." The dealer drew another card, flipped it and said, "Dealer shows a seven, looks like you're on a streak there sir." Player Two nodded, his smile never fading as he pulled the chips toward his three stacks.

I decided it was time to do something besides watch, and laid a hundred-dollar bill on the table. "I'm in," I said. The dealer looked at me with a puzzled expression. Normally at the hundred-dollar tables the players threw in enough money to play a few hands at a stretch. She slid a chip toward him and said, "Welcome to the game, sir." Player One stammered, "I . . . I think . . . I'll sit this one out." Player Two never looked up from the table and slid a stack of five chips to the betting line. The dealer flipped him two cards, then two more to me. She took two cards and showed her up card was a Jack. Player two had a Queen and a four and tapped the table for another card. I was showing my ten and nine and said, "Stay." Player Two lifted the edge of his new card, and still smiling, flipped it over. It was a seven. The dealer showed her down card, a ten, and said, "Another winner for the man with the smile."

I just stood there, frozen and speechless. Any other time a hand of nineteen would have been a winner but today was like a gambler's day in hell; close every time but no winners to show for it. The dealer looked at me and asked, "Another hand, sir?" I stood for a moment, thinking about the two-hundred dollars I still had in my wallet. Finally, I shook my head and said, "No . . . I'm done." I walked slowly back toward the entrance lobby. "Holy shit," I thought, "I lost a thousand bucks in two and a half hours." I had felt the same kind of loser's pain before but never to this degree. Not only was my loss a big one, it never would have happened if I hadn't stolen the money from the bank. Stolen money, lost at a casino and someone else was going to get stuck with the crime. "What in hell was I thinking?" I muttered as I walked outside.

The drive home seemed to happen in a fog of guilt and remorse. When I pressed the button on my garage door opener it occurred to me that I hadn't remembered a thing about the half hour drive from the casino. By 5:30 I was sprawled on the sofa, a beer in one hand and the remote control in the other, mindlessly clicking between college football games, not caring who was playing or winning. My mind wandered to the two thousand dollars in the manila envelope under the mattress. "What if I try just one more time?" I thought, staring at my beer bottle. "My luck has to change sometime." The ring of my cellphone broke my train of reckless thought and I picked it up from the coffee table. It was Jenna, and I couldn't help but think, "Thanks, babe."

We talked for fifteen minutes and I started feeling more upbeat despite my depressing afternoon. I still had Jenna's money and I hoped she would be understanding when I told her that I had gambled to get the money back. I would accompany the lie with a promise to stop gambling, and this time I would swear that I meant it. If I ever doubted that

I had a gambling addiction, my losing afternoon and the circumstances that led to it convinced me that I needed help. And I knew it would be easier to handle when Jenna got home.

Sunday was a day of working in the yard, watching a few NFL games and getting ready for the work week ahead. Neither the TV news nor the morning newspaper mentioned anything about the bank robbery, but I couldn't help but dwell on it and wonder what John Doe was doing on his own beautiful Sunday afternoon.

7

I decided to skip my usual drive-time Starbucks stop and drove directly to the office. Between the robbery aftermath and the stress with Jenna, I had fallen behind some things at work and spent the day in the office trying to get my head back above water. I didn't leave the office until 6:30 and on my way home stopped at Chili's for a beer and a sandwich. After a few minutes I asked the bartender to turn one of the TV screens to local news, and after a few more minutes I felt a chill run down my back. The headline graphic on the newscast read *"**Bank Robber Caught**"*. The bar was noisy and I leaned forward, trying to hear the newsman but the bartender had kept the volume turned down low. I watched the report and saw the robber, or, rather, saw myself, on the bank videotape. The scene switched to a courtroom where John Doe, without his wraparound shades and black clothes, wearing an orange, County-issued prison jumpsuit, was standing with his head bowed as an arraignment judge read him the charges against him. It was the first time I had ever seen John Doe without his normal slicked back hair and wraparound shades and I felt queasy. The reporter said the suspect's name was John Patterson.

The late news on Channel 12 gave more details on the arrest and I watched it intently. They again showed the security camera video and the reporter used the term *"Starbucks Bandit"* as if it was some kind of clever tag given to a man who they didn't realize was completely innocent. Obviously, my coffee cup clue had worked. I stared at the screen even after a commercial came on. I wondered what was going through John Patterson's mind. What was his family feeling? Had his boss made the decision to fire him yet? What was he going through on his first night in the County lock-up?

I sat back on the sofa and stared at the ceiling, trying to remember my EVIDENCE IN and EVIDENCE OUT lists that I created when I conceived my plan. After I gave it some thought, the silver gray Toyota, the hidden note in the legal pad and the knowledge of the personalized coffee flavor seemed like scant proof that John Doe, or John Patterson didn't commit the crime. What if I sent that information to the police and they simply chose to ignore it? I felt sick to my stomach. I knew I had to come up with something that would get Patterson off the hook and I had to do it fast. Jenna would be back home tomorrow and my little bank caper charade would be impossible to continue. I sat there churning things over and over in my head and then it dawned on me that I just might have more evidence in Patterson's favor than I initially thought.

I hurried out to the garage, opened the lid to a large gray trash barrel in the corner and fished out the blue zipper bag I had hoped would disappear with the weekly garbage. Surely the police would show it to the bank teller and she'd recognize it. I also pulled out the wraparound sunglasses and jar of hair gel but immediately wondered how they could possibly be used to sway the opinion of the investigators. "Nope," I thought, "that would be pointless, I'll just stick to the original plan and throw in the bag for good measure. That's gotta get their attention."

Over several glasses of red wine, I carefully typed the note to the police that I hoped would get John Patterson out of jail. If you haven't already noticed it," I wrote, "go back exactly fifteen pages in the yellow legal pad and you'll see my message to you. I wrote it and then planted it under Patterson's front seat." That sounded good to me, because no one but the real perpetrator could know about the pad, let alone a hidden message. Then I wrote, "The Starbucks drink that was left on the teller counter was a Tall vanilla cinnamon latte." Again, it was an important bit of evidence that hadn't been presented in the news reports. Finally, I wrote, "Here is the bag that the teller filled for me." That would be the clincher, a piece of physical evidence right from the scene of the crime. How could the police disregard something like that? There was still the videotape from the security cameras but could that possibly be enough to convict a man?

Before I pulled the note from my printer I went back out to the garage and grabbed another pair of latex gloves. I put them on and then, standing at the kitchen counter I methodically cleaned every inch of the blue bag, inside and out, with disinfectant wipes. I figured they would not only remove any trace of my fingerprints but also perspiration, oil from my hands and any other minute sign that I had ever touched the bag. When I was finished I placed the note into the bag and then the bag into a large padded mailing envelope. After finding the address for the police station on the City's website I wrote it on the envelope in big, black letters along with the notation RE: BANK ROBBERY. On my way to work the next morning, and again wearing latex gloves, I dropped the envelope into the drive-through mailbox at the post office. I felt a palpable sense of relief. The note with all of the robbery details and the bag that held the money should set the wheels in motion and clear John Patterson's name.

8

As soon as I pulled up to the curb at the Arrivals area I saw Jenna's beautiful, smiling face in the crowd of people waiting for their rides home. Her smile was a pleasant surprise and it immediately eased my nervousness. Through the windshield she looked like a totally different woman than the grim, silent one

I had dropped off just a week before. I opened the driver-side door and carefully dodged the chaos of three lanes of entering and exiting traffic as I made my way back to the back of my Escape. I had no sooner lifted the hatch door when I saw Jenna standing beside me. Her arms enveloped me before I could say a word and our kiss lasted long enough for the car behind us to honk its horn as a reminder that other people were waiting to pull up to the curb too.

The drive home was a mix of chatter about Jenna's mother and some new projects I was close to getting under contract. All in all, our arguing and the stress related to my gambling seemed like a long-ago problem. I waited until after we finished dinner to bring up the subject of my being able to pay her back the money I took from her trust fund. When I handed her the envelope of cash she looked at it and gave me a half-hearted thank you, then told me she wished the money hadn't come from a win at the casino. We talked things over for awhile and I assured her that I was going to try hard to stay away from the tables. She looked at me with more than a little bit of doubt on her face but I meant what I said. If she had known where the money really came from the blackjack tables would sound like a good thing to her.

When Jenna went into the bedroom to finish unpacking I turned on the TV and searched the channels for news on the trial. After what seemed like an unending stream of commercials I finally found a report on Channel 12. The trial had begun but the reporter didn't mention any details of the case or the evidence. They played the same security camera video that had been played constantly since the arrest was made and the crawl at the bottom of the screen ran the term STARBUCKS BANDIT again. Jenna walked into the room and glanced at the screen but didn't seem to be interested. I tried to maintain the appearance of being disinterested in the story even when Becky the barista was shown testifying. It was obvious that the partially empty cup I had left on the teller counter was a piece of evidence and Becky must have been called to testify that it was John Doe's standing order. I couldn't help but wonder what other evidence would be presented.

Over the next few days life slowly returned to normal. Jenna went back to work at the ad agency, my workload was returning to a hectic but reassuringly secure pace and, overall, things felt pretty much routine. Of course, I kept one eye and one ear on any news of the trial. I checked the morning newspaper, drive-time news on the car radio and the local TV stations to look for any mention of the evidence against Patterson. The only things that were reported were an eyewitness who saw a small silver gray car that was similar to the one John Patterson drove speeding away from the bank and through the parking lot at the approximate time of the robbery and the Starbucks cup left at the scene. What about the note and the yellow legal pad? What about the blue nylon bag? Did my note have any effect on the way the police viewed the case?

The trial was recessed over the weekend and on my Monday lunch hour I got my first update on the case in four days. What I heard sent a chill down my spine. The prosecution had wrapped up its case and closing arguments were underway. The reporter said that the District Attorney's office felt confident they would get a conviction and the case would be handed to the jury by Tuesday afternoon. The fact the District Attorney was feeling confident told me that my note and the blue bag had no effect whatsoever on the way they viewed their case against John Patterson. Maybe they thought Patterson had arranged for a friend to send the note and the bag to make it look like someone else did the robbery. Or maybe they simply thought the videotape was overwhelming proof of Patterson's guilt, and the little Starbucks cup was the icing on the cake.

I didn't accomplish a damned thing for the rest of the day. My head was full of images of Patterson being led away to prison and of his family's tearful pleading to the judge. How could I have been so stupid, so naïve to think I could pull this off with no one suffering the consequences? I knew I had to do something and I had to do it soon, something that was guaranteed to screw up the DA's case, but what could I possibly do to counter the evidence? The videotape clearly showed a man who looked like Patterson enter, rob and exit the bank. That videotape was the foundation of the prosecution's case and the only way to alter the outcome was to discredit the tape. It wasn't exactly a struggle to figure out what I had to do. The STARBUCKS BANDIT had to make one more appearance.

On Tuesday morning Jenna and I went through our usual workday routine and were out the door and into our commutes to our respective offices by 7:30 AM. Instead of going to the office I called my assistant and told her I had a breakfast meeting with a developer and wasn't sure when I'd be in. Then I turned around and headed back home. It only took me about twenty minutes to change into my black shirt and slacks, slick back my hair with the gel and put on the wraparound shades. As I looked at myself in the bathroom mirror all I could think was, "Man, I saw you on tape on the TV."

The TV report on Monday said the trial was supposed to resume at 9:00 AM. I headed downtown and had to circle the courthouse area twice before I could find a parking space. At 9:42 I paused, took a deep breath, slowly pushed open the doors at the rear of the courtroom and walked in. I stood there scanning the public seating area for an empty chair and noticed a murmur of hushed voices spreading through the courtroom. I spotted an available chair and headed toward it and saw that everyone in the row of seats was staring at me. I glanced toward the front of the courtroom and saw the members of the jury looking at me. One of them, a gray haired man with horn-rimmed glasses looked totally confused. The female juror sitting beside him was wide-eyed, her hand clasped tightly over her mouth. I saw the prosecuting team staring at me and as I finally sat down I saw Becky the barista looking at me with an expression of utter shock. I saw John Patterson and for the first time I looked into his eyes. He looked like he had seen a ghost.

I tried hard not to show any sign of emotion or recognition of the disruption I had caused but it didn't take more than about thirty seconds for the judge to point toward me and say, "Bailiffs, please escort the tall gentleman in the sunglasses to my chambers immediately. And the prosecution and counsel for the defense please join us as well. Court is in recess for thirty minutes."

The same queasiness and near-panic that hit me when I walked through the doors of the bank hit me again, only harder. This was like my own personal point of no return. From the very beginning of my little plot I believed I could pull off the heist and also get the innocent suspect off the hook. It was a simple plan with a simple solution but, as usual, the fucking lawyers got involved and made it complicated. I stood up as the two bailiffs approached me. One of them took me firmly by my right arm and steered me down the aisle toward the judge's bench while the other one followed behind me. It's strange how a simple thing like that can make a person feel like a criminal. We made a right turn at the bench and went through a large, mahogany door into the judge's chamber. A bronze sign on the door read HON. MAURICE SCOVILLE, 3ᴿᴰ DISTRICT COURT.

One of the bailiff's remained in the corridor while the other one led me to a chair in front of Judge Scoville's desk and then said firmly, "Remain standing until you are told to sit." To say I was scared shitless would be more than an understatement and I stood silently, looking around at the faces of the judge and the attorneys as they all gathered around the desk. Finally, Judge Scoville sat down in his huge, green leather chair, glared at me and said "You may sit now." The attorneys remained standing while the court reporter adjusted her chair in front of a small desk in the corner of the room. There was a very long and very uncomfortable silence before the judge finally said, "Please remove your sunglasses and identify yourself." I took of my shades, cleared my throat and answered, "Brad . . . Bradley Michael Chase, your honor." "So, Mr. Chase," he continued, "would you please tell us all what in the hell you had in mind when you walked into this courtroom today." The harsh edge of his voice made it clear that he was more than a little upset. I looked around the room to see if I could pick up on the mood and I did, it was one bunch of very angry and tense-looking people staring back at me.

"Well sir," I started, "I guess whatever it was I was thinking was kind of dumb. I've been watching the news lately and saw how much I resembled the guy on trial so I dressed up like him and came here today to watch the trial." Judge Scoville looked at me over the top of his wire framed glasses, his glare never diminishing and he asked, "Mr. Chase, how old are you?" "I'm thirty-eight." "Okay, you're thirty-eight and you think this juvenile little masquerade is somehow amusing, is that it?" "Well, I really didn't do it to be funny, I guess I was just curious about what might happen." Before Scoville could continue, one of the attorneys interrupted, "Your Honor, I have worked very hard on building a case against the defendant and we have felt all along we could get a conviction, but I'm afraid that this little stunt that Mr. Chase has pulled today will put doubt in the jury's minds, a reasonable doubt as to Mr. Patterson's identity and involvement in the robbery." Scoville leaned back in his chair and ran his hand over his wrinkled face. "I agree Mr. Portman," he said," and to be honest if I were one of the jurors and I saw Mr. Chase walk into the courtroom the way he did I would have doubts, very strong doubts about everything I saw on the bank's videotape."

"Your Honor," Portman said softly, "may I have a word with you in private please?" "Yes, certainly, but I'd like the defense team to be part of it," Scoville answered as he motioned to the bailiff. I was led into a small connecting staff office and told to wait there. I sat in a small, wobbly wooden chair for about ten minutes, wondering what was happening on the other side of the door. Portman seemed worried that his case against Patterson was in jeopardy and that was exactly my reason for being in the courtroom in the first place. It was a big gamble on my part, trying to confuse the jurors by showing them a second John Patterson. I knew there was still the physical evidence to deal with but if the identity of the man shown on the video was called into question the prosecution's case would be flimsy at best. In my mind I walked back through every detail of the robbery, the evidence, the note I had sent to the police, all of it. I couldn't think of any holes in my plan but that didn't do anything to ease my worries about what still might happen. Finally, the bailiff opened the door and told me to come back into the judge's chambers.

Judge Scoville was sitting at his desk, leaning forward with his hands folded in front of him. Attorney Portman and his assistant sat grim faced at a small, round table. The defense attorney's expression was anything but grim, it was almost serene, as though a great weight had been lifted from his shoulders. The bailiff moved a chair away from the attorney's table and set it in front of the judge's desk and then motioned for me to sit in it. Even though I was nervous I felt strangely confident as well. Judge Scoville, still leaning forward, looked directly at me and asked, "Mr. Chase, did you send a message to the police department about evidence in this case?" I wasn't expecting the question but I swallowed, and then answered, "No sir." I tried to convey an expression of confusion. "And Mr. Chase, do you own a blue nylon cash deposit bag?" Again, I tried to appear confused and said, "No sir I don't." Portman interrupted, "What kind of car do you drive Mr. Chase?" I turned toward him and said, "A 2011 Ford Escape, a red one." Portman wrote something on a notepad while his assistant whispered something to him. As he had from the beginning of the meeting the defense attorney remained silent. Then Portman asked, "Do you and the defendant, Mr. Patterson, know one another?" Again I answered, "No sir."

"Mr. Chase," Scoville said in a voice tinged with anger, "despite your little stunt today this trial will proceed as planned. Right now there is no way to determine what, if any, damage you might have caused to the trial but it is my intention to do everything possible to ensure that justice is served." He leaned back in his chair and stared at me for a moment before saying,

"And I will also tell you that Mr. Portman and I discussed bringing a contempt of court charge against you." I felt that same queasy feeling again. Any kind of charges like that would mean Jenna would find out about my interest in the case along with my disguise and that would surely lead to questions about the envelope of cash I gave her. I swallowed hard and waited for Scoville to finish his comment. Portman finished it for him. "Fortunately for you we decided against it but I have to tell you that something doesn't smell right here. This is all just a little too cute and a little too contrived. A bank was robbed and we believe we know who did it." He left that comment floating in the silence of the room and I struggled to avoid showing any kind of reaction. Judge Scoville stood up and said, "Mr. Chase, please see my assistant in the outer office to your right. We want your name, address and phone number in the event we want to question your further. I definitely didn't like the sound of that but I nodded and said, "Yes sir."

9

The evening news that night mentioned that the trial was unexpectedly recessed earlier in the day but resumed later and the case was now in the hands of the jury. Apparently my stunt had little or no effect on the pace of the trial and I hoped it wasn't an indication that it had no effect on the jurors as well. I remembered how worried Attorney Portman had seemed when he talked about reasonable doubt and how Judge Scoville had shared his concern. It would only take one juror to turn the decision, one person who, after a week of seeing John Patterson on the videotape saw me walk into the courtroom looking like an exact double. I didn't know if the jurors would work into the evening or break until the morning so I kept the TV on all evening, constantly clicking around to find any kind of update. Jenna asked me why I was so interested in the trial and all I could come up with was because I also liked Starbucks. It was a lame answer but Jenna seemed to accept it.

The next day at the office I found myself lingering in front of the TV in the lobby but it wasn't until my lunch hour while I was running a few errands that I heard the news on the radio. John Patterson was off the hook because of a hung jury. The jury foreman was interviewed on-air and said the group was hopelessly deadlocked at nine for conviction and three for acquittal. The judge had no choice but to declare a mistrial and said that according to state law Patterson could not be tried again for the crime. I felt a sense of relief I hadn't felt since I first began to concoct my robbery scheme. It had always been my intention to keep an innocent man from going to jail and I felt bad that Patterson had to endure the pain of the accusations and everything the trial brought his way. But as relieved as I was I couldn't stop thinking about the things that the judge and prosecutor had said. How things looked too cute and contrived. How the whole thing didn't smell right. And the words that really hit him hard were when Portman said they knew who did it. Did they suspect me or think Patterson and I were in it together? Why did the judge say they might want to ask me more questions?

When I got back to my office I closed the door, took out a pen and notepad and started to list any things that could be considered loose ends that I should tie up. The first thing that came to mind was Jenna's car. If the police found out that her Nissan bore a strong resemblance to Patterson's Toyota it would throw up a red flag that would make them look into things farther. If they talked to Jenna and found out she was out of town when the robbery occurred they would know her car was available for me to use. That would also make Jenna wonder how, within days of the bank robbery, I just happened to find enough luck at the casino to win her money back. That could lead to a discussion about my gambling addiction and a plausible motive for me to turn to robbery as a solution to my losses. So it was the car, the cash and Jenna's trip out of town that were problematic. It was a short list and the longer I looked at it and thought about it the clearer the solution became. The silver gray car would be the trigger to ask more questions but without a connection to it Jenna would be of no interest to the police. Get rid of the Nissan and the police hit a brick wall with their questions. It was obvious what I needed to do but convincing Jenna to get rid of a three year old car that was paid for and ran great would be a challenge, but if I could pull it off I could breathe easy again.

That evening while Jenna and I shared an after-dinner glass of wine, a commercial for the entry level Audi coupe came on the TV and I used it to bring up the subject of a new car. "That's a great looking little car," I said. Jenna watched for a moment and said, "Yeah, it sure is." "You'd look good in that," I continued,." "Yeah, and I'd have to get a new wardrobe if I drove an Audi," she laughed. "Seriously though," I said, "I know you aren't crazy about the Nissan, you think it looks stodgy." "It *is* stodgy and it's also inexpensive, economical and paid for." I couldn't tell if I was making any progress but I kept the subject going. The final shot of the commercial was a banner that said "PRICES SLASHED—ZERO PERCENT FINANCING". "You know babe," I said, "you work hard and you deserve to drive something you can be proud of, not embarrassed." Jenna looked at me, eyebrows raised and said, "Honey, that's an expensive car you're talking about." "No not really, it's their base model," I said, "and besides, you'd get a great trade-in on your Nissan and the bonus I'm getting for closing the deals on those two school projects will make a great down payment. I'd really like to do this for you, babe, especially after all you've had to put up with from me."

After another half hour of conversation about the car and some quick figuring on a calculator, we agreed to get the Audi. Jenna said she would leave her office early to stop by the dealer and look at the A4 coupe. The selection would be hers to make and I would get things rolling on the financing end of things. Two days later everything was in place and we agreed to drive together in the Nissan on Saturday morning to pick up the new car. Jenna was excited about her new wheels and I was eager to get the only remaining bit of evidence out of my garage.

The rest of the work week dragged by, mainly because I was still thinking about the judge's comments and the fact he held out the possibility of questioning me further. The trial was over and I hoped the investigation was too. All I could do was assume that no news was good news. On Saturday morning I got up early and spent a half hour emptying out the trunk and glove box of the Nissan. I put everything into a cardboard box and assumed Jenna would load most of it into the Audi when we got home. I took a quick shower and told Jenna I was heading to Starbucks and would bring her back a cup of coffee. I drove my Escape and stopped on the way to fill my tank and do a drive-through wash. When I got to Starbucks the place was unusually empty for a Saturday, and as usual Becky was behind the counter.

"Hi Brad, how are you?" she asked in her usual cheerful voice. "Hi Becky, I'm doing fine thanks, how about you?" The words were no sooner out of my mouth when I regretted saying them. I should have remembered that asking her anything about her personal life usually resulted in a torrent of minutia and silliness, just like her sick cat story, and I figured her involvement in the trial would be topic number one. She didn't disappoint. "Oh, I'm fine I guess, now that the trial is over. Did you know about the trial? It was for John who comes in here all the time and they said he robbed the bank next door but I didn't think he did it and it turned out they let him go." "Yeah," I muttered. "I heard about that, and then ordered my two cups of coffee." "Well," she continued, "they found one of our cups in the bank and brought it over and I was working so they asked me if I knew anyone who ordered a tall vanilla latte with cinnamon and I said John ordered one every day." "Really," I asked, playing dumb, that's interesting." "Yeah, and they even made me testify in court. I felt so bad because John is such a nice guy but I'm glad he got off." "I decided to do a little bit of fishing to see what else might have been said in court."

"I heard on the news they had videotape of him at the bank" I said cautiously, "did you see it?" Yeah, I did, and I thought it was John but then the other day this guy walked into the courtroom and he looked just like John and everybody got all surprised and confused and they recessed the court and led the guy into the judge's office and then after a while they started the trial again. I nodded, figuring she was finished as she handed me my order. She rang it up and I paid her, and just as I started to say goodbye she said, "Um, Brad, I don't know if I should say this but a police investigator was here again yesterday and he . . . he asked me if I knew you . . . and I told him yes." I tried not to show the panic that suddenly hit me and asked, "Why did they want to know that?" "I don't know, they didn't say. They just wanted to know if you were a customer and if you had a regular order and if I knew if you and John were friends." A line of four people had formed behind me and the conversation wasn't exactly on a topic I wanted to share with the public. I gave Becky a quick good bye and headed back to the car. Driving back to my house, I knew that, more than ever, it was important to ditch the Nissan.

I pulled into the garage and took Jenna's coffee to her as she finished getting dressed. "Give me two minutes," she said. I told her I'd back the Nissan out of the garage and wait for her there, "Are you excited about the car?" she asked. "Excited doesn't begin to describe it," I answered, trying to smile. I got into the Nissan, backed it into the middle of the driveway and turned on the radio. "Come on Jenna," I thought to myself, "let's get going." I looked at my watch. Her two minutes had turned to ten and I was thinking of going back into the house to hurry her up when a reflection caught my eye in the outside mirror. I turned to look and saw a police cruiser with two men in it pulling up to the curb behind me.